'Twas ...
C ...

Unlike the rhym... ...
rarely have the luxury of quiet moments, but
whichever ward or clinic is involved they all
share in the anticipation and excitement
building up to the joys of Christmas Day.

Our four books this month are set in hospitals
during Christmas Eve, when emotions are
heightened, and our heroes and heroines are,
unexpectedly or not, forced to confront their
real feelings. We visit Casualty, Maternity,
Intensive Care and Paediatrics, and in the dark
hours of the night touch on sadness, humour
and joy, before facing the dawn of a wonderful
new day.

Merry Christmas!

Margaret Barker pursued a variety of interesting careers before she became a full-time author. Besides holding a degree in French and Linguistics, she is a Licentiate of the Royal Academy of Music, a State Registered Nurse, and a qualified teacher. Happily married, she has two sons, a daughter and an increasing number of grandchildren. She lives with her husband in a sixteenth-century thatched house near the East Anglian coast.

Recent titles by the same author:

HERO'S LEGACY
HOME-COMING
I'D LOVE A BABY!

CAROL'S CHRISTMAS

BY
MARGARET BARKER

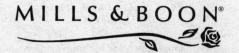

MILLS & BOON®

First published in Great Britain 1998
Harlequin Mills & Boon Limited,
Eton House, 18-24 Paradise Road, Richmond, Surrey TW9 1SR

© Margaret Barker 1998

ISBN 0 263 81254 5

Set in Times Roman 10½ on 11½ pt.
03-9812-50489-D

Printed and bound in Norway
by AIT Trondheim AS, Trondheim

CHAPTER ONE

'YOU know, of course, he's back?' Fay said, in as casual a voice as she could muster under the highly sensitive circumstances.

'Who?'

Carol knew perfectly well that her friend was referring to the man who was, invariably, uppermost in her mind, but she needed time to gather her composure.

'Euan,' Fay said quietly, her eyes anxiously searching Carol's face to judge her reaction.

'Yes.' Carol's voice quavered as she made her reply. Her fingers trembled as she dropped the hospital badge she was pinning to her royal blue uniform dress and sank onto the nearest chair.

Fay ran her hands through her short, dark hair. 'I thought you would know.' She cleared her throat nervously. 'In fact, I secretly hoped that was why—' She broke off in embarrassment. 'I think I'll make some strong coffee.'

Carol leaned against the back of her chair and looked up at the mistletoe, strategically placed above Sister Fay Gordon's desk. Garlands of brightly coloured paper chains intertwined with holly festooned the small office.

She closed her eyes as the memory of that fateful Christmas, two years ago, forced itself upon her. It was even more vivid with her eyes shut so she quickly opened them again and watched Fay as she busied herself with the kettle and the jar of instant coffee.

'What did you secretly hope, Fay?' she asked quietly.

Fay placed two steaming mugs on her desk and looked

5

across at Carol. 'I assumed you knew Euan was our new consultant in Accident and Emergency and—'

'No! I knew Euan was back at the Moortown General but I didn't know he was a consultant and I certainly didn't think he'd be working here in Accident and Emergency.'

The full implication of Fay's words hit Carol like a blast from an explosion. How would she cope when she had to work alongside him? And how would Euan react when he found out she was working in his department? She felt utterly shell-shocked as she stared wide-eyed at her friend.

Fay picked up her coffee-mug, cradling it in her hands as if for support. 'Euan's been the consultant in my department for the past week. I assumed you knew and that was why—'

'So you were secretly hoping I was here for a reconciliation, were you?' Carol breathed.

Fay sipped her coffee, watching Carol intently. 'Something like that. After all, we haven't seen hide or hair of the pair of you for nearly two years and then you both turn up during the same week, so...'

Carol crossed her arms defensively in front of her. 'Actually, I've come up to Moortown to have a discussion about whether to proceed with our divorce,' she said in a firm voice that belied the butterflies flapping around in the pit of her stomach. She took a sip of her coffee as she tried to steady her nerves.

'I left a message on Janet's answerphone as soon as I arrived in Moortown yesterday, but she hasn't got back to me yet. It was Janet who, in her capacity as my solicitor, arranged the official separation order two years ago. She contacted me last month to say the two-year separation was nearly up and asked if I wanted to proceed with the divorce.'

She swallowed the lump in her throat. If only she knew what the right course of action was. If only she knew how Euan felt about her since their awful break-up and the two-year separation. This was why she'd had to travel north to find out.

She looked across the desk at Fay, who was adjusting the white cuffs on her navy blue sister's uniform.

'Oh, Janet will be a tower of strength, Carol,' Fay said quickly, obviously trying to defuse the tense atmosphere. 'She's got an excellent professional reputation here in Moortown. Funny to think of the three of us at school together! We had some good times, didn't we? Remember the time the whole class hid in those empty cupboards when the new biology mistress came into the lab?'

Carol smiled back, momentarily forgetting her problems as she remembered the fun they'd had together at school.

'I don't think Miss Pincher was amused.'

'An understatement, if I remember rightly,' Fay said wryly. 'You'll be OK with Janet as your solicitor. But I can't help feeling sorry that you separated in the first place. I mean…'

Carol put both hands against her flushed cheeks. 'Fay, it simply wasn't working out between us. For the last six months before we split we never stopped arguing and—'

'Have you seen Euan since you left him?'

Carol swallowed hard. 'No!' She drew in her breath, trying to banish the familiar pain.

'I wrote to give him a forwarding address when I became a sister with the cruise line, and he wrote to me when he moved to London so that when we needed to get in touch by letter or fax we could. There were a few official letters we had to decide between us and so on, but, no…we haven't seen each other.'

Haven't even spoken on the phone.

For some unknown reason she remembered the postcard she'd sent Euan when she'd been in Bali, having a couple of precious hours away from the ship on which she was working. She'd been sitting under a palm tree when a young boy had approached her and asked her to buy something from him. After buying a colourful batik sarong, she'd had the urge to write to Euan so she'd bought a postcard which the boy had produced from the bottom of his basket.

It had been such an idyllic spot she'd longed to share it with Euan—not with the Euan of the last six months before they'd separated—the Euan she'd first fallen in love with. And there and then she'd dashed off a postcard full of banal phrases like, 'Hope you are well.'

It had been the one and only unnecessary communication between them in the whole of the two years.

Euan hadn't replied. What had there been to reply to? He hadn't known how she'd been feeling at the time, missing him so dreadfully, aware that although her life had been full of excitement and important professional commitment Euan had never been far from her thoughts.

She bent to retrieve her hospital badge from the tiled floor, preparing to fix it, with trembling fingers, into her staff nurse's uniform. The news that Euan and she would be actually working together had affected her more than she cared to admit, even to herself. She'd hoped to get in touch with him but only for a short time when he was off duty to find out how he felt about proceeding with the divorce.

'Ouch!' A trickle of blood ran down the index finger of her left hand as she inadvertently stabbed herself.

'Here you are,' Fay said quickly, pushing a box of

tissues across the desk. 'Don't worry. I've got more spare uniforms in the box that the laundry room delivered when we sent out our appeal for temporary staff.'

'It's OK. The blood's on my hand, not the dress.' Carol gave a wry smile. 'I notice you let me fix myself into a uniform before you dropped your bombshell. Where do you keep your small adhesive plasters?'

Fay put her head on one side as she smiled back. 'I didn't want to risk losing you. Trained nurses are hard to come by at short notice, especially Moortown General trained.'

She pointed across the room. 'Small plasters in that cupboard over there.'

Carol wrapped a piece of tissue round her finger and crossed the room in the direction Fay was waving. She didn't hear the door opening as she selected a small plaster and returned to the desk to drop the bloodstained tissue in the bin.

'How's the recruitment campaign going, Fay?' someone said, behind her back.

She heard the deep, gravelly voice but at first nothing registered with her. A feeling of unreality swept over her. She could feel her legs turning to jelly as she turned to face her estranged husband. She saw the grey eyes widen with disbelief as he stared at her. For a moment neither of them spoke.

It was Euan who broke the silence. 'You're still bleeding, Carol. Here, let me do that.' He took the plaster from her shaking fingers, peeling back the gauze.

'What on earth were you trying to do to yourself?' he said, his usually confident voice quavering.

She caught a whiff of his distinctive aftershave as he bent his head to fix the plaster round her finger. Coupled with the unnerving touch of his fingers, she was momentarily transported back to the time when they had been so close, in that far-away life that didn't exist any more. His dark brown hair was combed back away from his forehead, now wrinkled in concentration.

When Euan looked up he appeared to be totally in command of himself again.

It was as if she'd never been away, apart from the huge, invisible, emotional barrier they'd erected between them.

'Thanks,' she said, in a barely audible, croaking voice. 'I was pinning my hospital badge on and—'

'So what exactly are you doing here? I thought you'd be spending Christmas on one of your luxury cruise liners.'

'No, I'm helping out in Accident and Emergency because of the flu epidemic. I actually came up to Moortown to try and have a discussion with you. Janet wanted us to come to a decision and…'

He frowned. 'I told you in my letter that I was just starting a new job at the Moortown and I wouldn't have time to meet you until some time in the New Year. I presume you got my letter?'

'Of course I got your letter,' Carol said evenly. 'But I'll be travelling again in the New Year so I thought if we could get together for a discussion some time over Christmas…'

'And, like I told you in the letter, I'm working over Christmas and a discussion of this nature is going to take time,' he said firmly.

'Coffee, Euan?' Fay asked, quickly.

'Yes, please.'

He eased himself into one of the two armchairs and stretched out his long legs in front of him, crossing one highly polished shoe over the other.

Carol noticed the expensive cut of the grey woollen suit on his youthful, athletic figure. He was looking good, probably still running several miles a week to keep in trim. He didn't look thirty-seven, apart from the air of authority he seemed to have assumed since becoming a consultant.

She turned away, swallowing hard. He'd achieved his dream and it didn't include her. Perhaps it never had done. He'd always been motivated by the promise of success in his professional life.

She became aware that Fay was asking her if she wanted more coffee.

'Shouldn't I be starting work out there?' she said quickly.

'We're neither of us, theoretically, on duty until eight,' Fay said easily. She removed Carol's mug, spooned in more instant and topped it up from the kettle.

'Day Sister will be in here any minute to give her report and then it'll be all hands on deck. This is the calm before the storm so make the most of it. It may be Christmas Eve but it's business as usual in Accident and Emergency.'

'Thanks, Fay.' Carol picked up her coffee-mug and took a long sip. Her hands, she noticed thankfully, had stopped trembling. She felt almost in command of herself…until she looked across at Euan.

The door opened and Day Sister Jill Watson, a small, plump, capable-looking woman in her mid-forties, came in.

'Oh, am I too early, Fay? It's just that, being Christmas Eve, I want to get back to the family and…'

'Perfect timing, I would say, wouldn't you, Carol?' Fay said, shooting Carol a meaningful glance. 'Carol has kindly come in for the night in response to the appeal we put out over the local television news.'

'Ah, so you're just here for one night, then, Carol?' Euan said. He hauled himself to his feet and moved closer, looking down at her with that scrutinising expression that had always unnerved her in so many different ways in the past. She was sure she could detect a note of relief in his voice.

She looked up at him and her green eyes flickered as she met his gaze. For a moment she wished she hadn't had the coloured rinse put on her hair because she could see Euan's eyes, roving critically over it.

He didn't like anything artificial so during the last two years, almost as an act of defiance, her naturally auburn hair had been highlighted and lowlighted and had changed colour so frequently she'd had difficulty describing its original shade to the many ships' hairdressers who'd found her complete trust in their abilities so totally refreshing.

It was now a darker shade of auburn than her natural colour, cut to shoulder length with a fringe that touched her darkened eyebrows. The dark brown velvet band that supported the small hairpiece the hairdresser had fixed to heighten the crown of her hairdo suddenly felt constricting.

Adding to her feeling of emotional discomfort, her throat had become very dry when she started to explain why she was here.

She cleared her throat. 'Yes, there was I, preparing for a quiet Christmas Eve, watching TV, when up came this announcement about the flu epidemic here at Moortown General. Well, I couldn't ignore a cry for help from my old training hospital so here I am.'

In actual fact, the appeal had been a godsend to her. She'd been wondering how she could contact Euan and persuade him to meet her for a discussion, even though he'd written to say he couldn't possibly spare the time over Christmas.

'How very noble of you,' Euan said quietly, his grey

eyes moving from her hair to meet her gaze. 'Well, I'd better get on with some work.'

Carol tried to steady her rapid breathing as she watched him, striding towards the door.

'Oh , Mr Maitland, could you take a look at the small boy I've just settled in cubicle four?' Jill Watson asked, moving quickly to detain him.

Her plump, good-natured face puckered anxiously. 'Phil Morton, your senior registrar, is busy with another patient, your junior registrar has gone down with flu and Rod Grant and Geoff Bailey, the two housemen, are sorting out an injured motorcyclist. My staff nurse will fill you in on the case history.'

Euan paused by the door, an enigmatic expression on his face. 'I expect your nurse is wanting to go off duty, Sister Watson, so perhaps Staff Nurse would like to relieve her.'

Carol took a deep breath. She would have to go through with it even though she could see that Euan was plainly annoyed with her, for turning up unexpectedly. She was working here in the hospital for one night only and she was a professional.

'Yes, I'd like to start work,' she said quickly, glancing back at Jill Watson. 'Cubicle four, you said, Sister?'

Euan was actually holding open the door for her. He was being ultra-polite, ultra-gallant, in front of her two colleagues. She wondered how polite he would be when they were finally left alone to argue out their differences!

They'd said some very wounding things to each other on that Christmas Eve two years ago.

The door closed behind them and they were walking together along the row of cubicles. She thought fleetingly how little had changed since the time she'd worked in Accident and Emergency when she'd been a student nurse. The cream paint was newer and brighter and the treatment and resuscitation rooms, which Fay had briefly shown her when she'd arrived this evening, were better equipped and technologically more sophisticated, but the dear old Moortown General building was still the same.

The outside walls had been cleaned a couple of years ago but were gradually returning to the grey colour which blended in more naturally with the millstone grit buildings of this bleak Yorkshire town, dominated on every side by tall brown and green hills interspersed with vast moorland, stretching away as far as the eye could see.

Two years ago, before she'd resigned, she'd been Sister of Female Surgical Ward and patients had been brought to her from Accident and Emergency at frequent intervals. She'd never thought she would ever be working down here. It was a whole new experience but she was confident she could cope with it.

But it was going to be difficult, maintaining a professional relationship with Euan. It was a challenge which she hadn't envisaged.

Euan was pushing open the door of cubicle four. Following him inside, she saw a small, dark-haired boy in a blue, hand-knitted sweater and matching trousers, lying on his side on top of the white aertex blanket that covered the treatment couch. His little legs were curled up almost to his chin in the foetal position, and his eyes were tightly shut. Dried blood caked his right eyelid. His worried mother was holding his hand and speaking softly to him. She looked up expectantly when Carol and Euan arrived.

'Is he going to be all right, Doctor?' she asked, hesitantly, the strain of recent events showing in her wide-eyed gaze.

Euan sat down on the side of the couch below the little boy's feet. 'I'll be able to tell you more when I've had a look at him,' he said, gently. 'What's your boy's name?'

'Michael,' the mother said in a quavering voice.

The staff nurse handed Euan the case notes. His eyes scanned the page of notes before he turned and handed the file to Carol. She glanced at the notes, before suggesting to the staff nurse that she went off duty.

'Would you like to tell me what happened?' Euan asked the patient's mother gently.

The young woman ran a thin hand over her long dark hair and her features tensed as she recalled how she had taken her two small sons with her to the garden shed to search for a box of Christmas fairy lights which had gone missing. The boys had found some garden canes and had started a playful fight while she was still searching.

'As far as I can gather, Michael looked up at the wrong moment—just when Jonathan was pointing his stick towards him. He blinked automatically but the cane went through his closed eyelid and pierced the eyeball. The cane fell out so I don't think it can have gone in too far, Doctor, but...'

'Well, let's have a look, shall we?' Euan said in a reassuring voice as he put his hand gently on the little boy's arm.

'Michael, can you hear me?'

The little boy nodded ever so slightly, followed by a wincing gesture of pain.

Euan ran his hand over his patient's forehead in a soothing gesture. 'You're a brave little man, Michael. I'll give you something to make you feel better.'

He turned to take the notes from Carol and wrote up a painkilling injection.

'Will you take care of that, Staff Nurse?'

Carol nodded as she went out, carrying the notes with her.

In her office, Fay was just finishing taking the day report from Jill Watson. She unlocked the drugs cupboard and checked the required dosage. Seconds later Carol was back in cubicle four, administering the injection.

She was relieved to find that the fact that Euan was watching her didn't have any detrimental effect on her professionalism. When there was medical work to be done she simply had to switch herself off from their emotional trauma and get on with the job.

It was going to be OK. She would survive the night. Compared with the trauma that the young mother was going through, her own problems seemed unimportant.

The little boy hadn't moved as she'd given the injection. She glanced up at Euan, waiting to see what he planned to do next.

'I'm going to have to move you onto your back, Michael, so that I can take a look at your eye. Can you roll this way for me? That's a good boy...'

Euan had always had a winning way with children, Carol thought as she watched him. He would have made a good father. She deliberately obliterated the treacherous thought as soon as it presented itself, remembering how she'd argued her case for parenthood.

Determinedly shaking off the memories, she took hold of Michael's other hand, the one his mother wasn't holding. The little boy opened his good eye and looked up at her.

'Who are you?' he asked in a barely audible voice.

'I'm Carol,' she said gently.

A faint smile hovered on the little boy's lips. 'You mean, like a Christmas carol? We sang some at school.'

'Which was your favourite?' Carol asked, leaning forward.

Euan was focussing his ophthalmoscope, shining a light near the injured eye.

'Michael, will you tell us which is your favourite carol?' he asked quietly. 'And do you think you could open your eye while you're telling us?'

The injured eyelid opened slightly. Euan held it gently with his fingers as he examined the eyeball with the ophthalmoscope.

' I like that one about the little baby in the manger,' Michael whispered hesitantly. 'But I can't remember how it goes.'

He raised his small hand and tapped Carol on the arm. 'Can you remember that one, Carol? It's something about stars in the bright sky and cows and things like that.'

Carol smiled. 'Yes, I know the one you mean.' She started singing softly, '"Away in a manger…"'

Halfway through the second line Michael joined in. Euan, intent on his examination of the delicate eyeball, turned his head briefly and flashed Carol a grateful smile. She felt a rush of nostalgic emotion as she reached the words, '"The stars in the bright sky looked down where he lay…"'

Michael shut both eyes. 'Keep singing while I go to sleep, Carol.'

She looked across at Euan, wondering if he'd had time to make a diagnosis before Michael had succumbed to the effects of the painkilling and sedative injection.

Euan mouthed, 'Keep singing.'

It wasn't easy to keep going in front of Euan but she concentrated on her patient. If it eased the situation for Michael and his mother it was a small price to pay!

By the time she'd reached the third verse, the little boy had drifted off to sleep.

'So, what did you find, Doctor?' Michael's mother asked quietly.

'It's difficult to say at this early stage,' Euan said carefully, straightening and putting the ophthalmoscope back on the trolley.

'The surrounding tissues in the eye are affected so it will be some time before we can make an accurate diagnosis,' he said gently.

The young mother's shoulders hunched forward dejectedly.

Euan reached out and patted her arm. 'Try not to worry. We'll keep Michael in hospital for a few days until the swelling on the eyelid subsides. I'm going to start him on some healing drops but we won't put them in until we get him to the children's ward.'

The little boy stirred fitfully and opened his good eye. Carol noticed what a beautiful brown colour it was, and hoped fervently that the injured eye would heal without any permanent damage.

'Will you come with me, Carol?' Michael said, holding tightly to her hand.

She glanced at Euan.

'Carol will go with you to the ward, Michael, and then she'll have to come back here to help all the other patients,' Euan said gently.

'But I'll call in to see you before I go off duty in the morning,' Carol said softly.

The little boy gave a half-smile. One hand plucked at his blue woollen sleeve. He pulled away a small piece of fluff, rolled it in a ball and tossed it in the air.

'It's going to be Christmas in the morning,' he said quietly. 'Do you think Father Christmas will know where I am?'

'I'll get a message to him,' Michael's mother put in quickly, 'and arrange for him to bring your presents here.'

The little boy's smile widened. He closed both eyes and turned his head on the pillow. Within seconds he was asleep. Carol smoothed the dark strands of hair away from his forehead.

Going to the phone outside the cubicle, she rang Paediatrics. She was relieved to find there was a spare bed. Ann Threadgold, Sister in Charge, also agreed to fix up a bed in a side ward for Michael's mother.

'So, what are you doing down there in A and E, Carol?' Ann asked. 'Anything to do with the fact that Euan's back?'

'Sheer coincidence,' Carol said quickly. 'I'm here temporarily in answer to the television appeal for trained nurses.'

'Pull the other one!' came the jocular reply.

Carol took a deep breath. Why did everyone think that she and Euan would find it easy to bridge the yawning chasm between them?

'I'm on my way up with the patient, Ann,' she said quickly, and put down the phone.

Euan, emerging from the cubicle, gave her a pointed look. 'What was all that about? Is there a problem?'

'Not with the admission,' she said shortly. 'Everybody's trying to pry into our personal lives. They just haven't realised what a two-year separation can do to a marriage.'

She heard the hissing sound of the breath he sucked in between his strong white teeth. His grey eyes held a guarded, enigmatic expression as he looked down at her. She felt a rush of unnervingly nostalgic emotion, churning through her. He put one hand against the wall above her head as his eyes held hers.

'I sometimes have difficulty, realising it myself,' he said quietly.

Neither of them spoke for several seconds. Around them, the busy A and E unit continued to function. A porter, pushing a trolley, whizzed past between them and Carol, desperately aware of Euan's close proximity, looked away.

An ambulance was pulling up at the main entrance, and a porter and a nurse were hurrying to meet it. But in the midst of this business-as-usual situation Carol suddenly felt very unsure and vulnerable, especially with Euan's hand pressed against the wall above her head. It felt so unreal to be standing here with him, communicating on a friendly basis.

'It's so different to Christmas Eve two years ago, isn't it?' she said, half to herself, and flinched as she saw the flicker of sadness in his expressive eyes.

'I wouldn't ever want to go through that again,' he said quietly.

The newly arrived patient was being wheeled in from the ambulance. The paramedics were hurrying towards them.

'Get back from Paediatrics as soon as you can, Carol,' Euan said as he went over to examine the new patient.

She hurried away, her thoughts in turmoil. For a few brief moments she'd glimpsed the old Euan, the man she'd married, the man who'd swept her off her feet all those years ago. She'd adored him, worshipped him…

Hey, steady on! said the voice of cold reason in her head.

She clutched her patient's little hand tightly as they went up in the lift. Michael was sleeping fitfully, every now and then opening his good eye to check that his mother and Carol were still with him.

As the porter pushed the trolley along the corridor

towards the children's ward Carol was thinking that she would have to pull herself together and not get carried away by nostalgic, sentimental emotion. Did she really want to fan the flames of her love for Euan? Hadn't she tried desperately to forget him over the past two years?

And even if she did want to try and patch things up, how did Euan feel? He'd just admitted that he wouldn't ever want to go through that awful Christmas Eve again. With an effort she gave all her concentration to her patient.

Small, dark-haired Sister Ann Threadgold welcomed and took charge of Michael and his mother, leaving Carol free to go back to A and E.

She paused by the door to turn and take a last look at her little patient. Ann was lifting him onto one of the small beds. She felt totally reassured. Michael was in good hands.

In the centre of the ward she could see a tall Christmas tree, decorated with silver strands of tinsel, golden trinkets and lots of little brightly coloured presents. It would be fun in the morning to watch the children's faces as they unwrapped their presents.

She went out and walked down the corridor, stopping for a nostalgic moment outside Female Surgical. She could hear the sound of carol-singing coming from the choral group who always visited on Christmas Eve.

'''Once in Royal David's City...'''

She simply couldn't resist pushing the swing doors half open so that she could take a quick peep.

'Carol! How lovely to see you! What on earth are you doing here? Come in!'

Her erstwhile colleague, tall, red-haired Jennifer Batchelor, who'd taken over from Carol as Sister two years ago, having been her staff nurse, was standing just inside the ward, listening to the carol-singers.

'Can't stop, Jennifer,' Carol said quickly. 'I'm helping out in A and E for the night. Couldn't resist a peep at the old ward. See you later.'

She hurried away before the inevitable barrage of questions came.

Back in A and E, she found that the new patient had been wheeled into the treatment room. Fay was helping Euan to remove the bloodstained clothing from his legs but she handed Carol her scissors as soon as she arrived.

'Can you finish this, please? There's a woman in labour in cubicle three. Staff Nurse Gregs is with her. I want to check if we've time to get her up to Obstetrics or—'

'Sister!'

Short, fair-haired Hannah Gregs poked her head round the door. 'The baby's head is barely visible at the top of the birth canal and the mother's trying to push!'

CHAPTER TWO

'DOESN'T sound as if Fay will get her patient to Obstetrics in time,' Euan said, the tip of his tongue set firmly between his teeth as he set up a saline drip on his accident patient.

Carol glanced up at him and felt a momentary stab of nostalgia as she recognised Euan's typical stance of concentration. In the early months of their marriage he'd attempted a certain amount of DIY jobs, and it seemed as if he couldn't work unless his tongue was clamped firmly between his teeth. She remembered how she'd pointed it out to him and they'd laughed together about it.

On one occasion, he'd been attempting to fix some bookshelves in what they'd laughingly referred to as the sitting room. There had never been much time for sitting in their busy lives but that was what it was called. The piles of books stacked against the walls had been crying out to be housed so Euan had gone out and bought some planks of wood, nails, hammer and various other assorted items.

She'd pointed out that it would have been easier to buy ready-made bookshelves with instructions but Euan had insisted that it would be cheaper this way. When the shelves had collapsed as they'd started putting the books on them they'd both fallen about, laughing. One thing had led to another and...

The memory of that cosy evening was too poignant to contemplate—the love-making, the laughter...

Laughter! That was what had gone out of their marriage in the latter stages.

Looking at Euan now, so skilled in his surgical expertise, she couldn't imagine why his DIY had always been such a disaster! But he'd insisted on doing it because it was supposed to have saved them money.

She put down the scissors and removed the last remnants of the bloodstained jeans to expose the fractured tibia, protruding through her patient's skin. She could hear Fay, in the next cubicle, soothing her patient. They'd obviously decided to complete the delivery in A and E rather than risk a delivery in the corridor or the lift *en route* to Obstetrics.

Her own patient was stirring, the effect of the painkillers given by the paramedics at the scene of the crash wearing off. She took hold of the hand that wasn't fixed to the drip to give her patient a feeling of comfort.

His long, fair, matted hair was spread out over the pillow. His brow was unwrinkled so he was a young man—couldn't be more than about eighteen at the most. Alcohol fumes drifted up towards Carol as he began to speak in an indistinct, guttural voice.

'Where the hell am I?'

'You're in hospital,' Euan said. 'Would you like to tell me your name?'

'Brad Somers…and I don't like hospitals so I think I'll go home… Aagh!'

Carol helped Euan to restrain their patient from lifting himself up. The movement had given him a lot of pain. Euan injected a further dose of painkiller and sedative and the patient responded almost immediately, by falling back into a drunken sleep.

'We'll have to be quick in treating this one,' Euan told Carol quietly. 'The paramedics found him lying in the road with his motorbike on top of him. It's obvious that both the bones in his lower leg are broken.'

He was rubbing his chin with one hand, his eyes thoughtful.

'We both know how difficult it can be to fix these bones in the correct position for healing.'

Carol nodded. 'Have Orthopaedics been notified?' she asked.

Euan pushed out his lips, another familiar gesture which Carol remembered he always did when he was concentrating on what to do next.

'The entire team is tied up in Theatre with the victims of the car crash that happened earlier this evening so I'm going to work on Brad in the treatment room. I've asked for a porter— Here he is. Carol, go with the patient, clean up the wound and set out what we'll need to do a long leg plaster of Paris so that...'

He paused, a smile lighting up his tense features as the unmistakable sound of a baby, crying lustily, came through the partition from the cubicle next door.

'Sounds like the delivery was successful,' he said. 'I'd better take a look before I hand Mum and baby over to Obstetrics. I'll join you in the treatment room, Carol.'

Carol caught a glimpse of a red-faced, squalling infant and a tired but happy young mother with long, damp, blonde hair as she went past cubicle three.

Fay poked her head out, her face wreathed in smiles.

'It's a dear little girl, Carol. Isn't she beautiful?'

Carol paused for a moment to watch Fay hand the noisy baby to its proud mother.

'They're all beautiful,' she said, her voice suddenly faltering as the familiar yearning swept over her.

Her patient on the trolley was snoring loudly. She asked the porter to wait for a moment. Impulsively, she took a step inside the cubicle to get a better view of the baby. The mother looked up and smiled.

'Have you come to take us to the ward, Nurse?'

'No, I'm just admiring your baby, that's all,' Carol said quickly.

'A nurse from Obstetrics will be arriving to take you up there soon,' Fay told the mother. 'Ah, here she is…and Mr Maitland as well.'

Carol stepped out of the cubicle, placing one hand back on her patient's trolley, as Euan and the tall, blonde Obstetrics staff nurse arrived simultaneously. As she watched the staff nurse go into the cubicle she had the distinct feeling she recognised her from somewhere.

Where had she seen her before? Perhaps way back at school? Possibly someone she'd known as a child who'd grown up and now looked different but still retained some recognisable characteristics?

But there had been no sign of recognition on the Obstetrics staff nurse's face as she'd passed her just now so maybe she was mistaken.

There were so many memories from the past in this hospital!

She would have liked to have spent more time, admiring the new baby, but there was work to be done. And babies always made the subconscious longing feeling worse.

She looked down at her patient and deliberately blanked out the dreams that threatened to undermine her efficiency.

With his face in unconscious repose, his long, straggly fair hair spread over the pillow, Brad Somers looked like a child—a naughty child, she thought as once again the full effects of the alcohol fumes wafted up to her. She looked across at the porter.

'How stupid to drink all that alcohol and then get on a lethal weapon like a motorbike and drive off somewhere!' she said.

'It could have been worse,' the grey-haired porter said. 'He might have killed himself or some innocent bystander. Crazy, these young kids, but you can't tell 'em. Now, take my brother's lad...'

For the rest of the journey along the corridor Carol had to listen to a sad tale about motorbikes, which made her even more convinced of the dangers of this deadly form of transport in the hands of youngsters. If ever she had a son... She deliberately stopped herself pursuing that train of thought, concentrating all her attention on her patient.

In the treatment room she scrubbed up, donned a sterile gown, hat and mask and began to clean up the wound. Euan arrived, scrubbed up and put on sterile garments, before beginning the difficult task of setting the two fractured bones.

'Fortunately, we've got clean breaks across both of them,' he said, as he fixed the fractured ends into position. 'If we can get a union first time, we won't have to resort to further treatment. It's so important to fix the leg quickly in these cases. Any delay can cause problems later.'

Carol nodded in agreement as she fixed sterile jelonet gauze over the wound, before handing Euan the strip of plaster of Paris bandage which she had been soaking in water.

'The air bubbles have stopped rising,' she told him, 'so that one is ready to be applied.'

With one hand she put another bandage in the water container and with the other she helped Euan to maintain a firm hold on the injured leg.

On completing the plaster, Euan took a sharp knife and trimmed the edges. Looking across the table, he smiled at Carol.

'I feel cautiously optimistic about this leg,' he said. 'I think we may have fixed it in time.'

The young man was stirring again, waving his arms in the air and groaning.

'He's going to have a terrible hangover in a few hours,' Carol said.

'At least we've got the leg out of harm's way,' Euan said. He stretched out his gloved hand and patted Carol's.

Through the thin texture of the glove she felt a frisson of excitement and gave herself a mental ticking-off. It was an automatic gesture, meaning absolutely nothing to Euan. He was simply relieved to have finished a difficult task.

The swing doors opened and a porter and a staff nurse came in to collect their patient and take him to Orthopaedics Ward.

As the swing doors closed again Carol moved away from the table, peeling off her gloves before removing her hat and gown and stowing them away in the laundry bin in the ante-room.

'Do you think that kettle works?' Euan asked, appearing in the doorway of the ante-room and tossing his gown and hat after hers.

She looked in the direction of the kettle and gave a wry smile. 'Was that a hint, by any chance?'

He moved over to her side and smiled down at her. As the corners of his full, sensual mouth turned upwards, she saw the creases in his forehead straighten out. Quickly she moved away to fill the kettle at the sink, keeping a tight rein on her conflicting emotions.

'I know you always told me I drank too much coffee but it's my only vice,' he said in a whimsical tone, settling down on one of the wooden chairs and stretching his long legs in front of him.

She plugged in the kettle and turned round to face him. 'Your only vice?' she said in a joky voice. 'I wouldn't say that.'

His grey eyes had assumed a serious expression as he searched her face. 'What would you say?' he said, his voice quietly husky.

She hesitated. 'I would say...being sure that you're always right is a vice...of sorts,' she said quietly, realising that she was opening up old wounds.

'Isn't that a vice we both share?' he asked evenly. 'You have your point of view, I have my point of view and never the twain shall meet.'

The kettle was boiling. She reached into a cupboard and found a half-empty jar of instant coffee.

She turned to look at him. 'Do you still take it black and sugar-free?'

He nodded. She handed him the mug. Their fingers touched and again she felt as if she'd been scorched by a lighted match. She sat down and watched him drink. He was deliberately avoiding her eyes. It had been like this two years ago on that fateful Christmas Eve. Both waiting for the other to make a move.

'You know, you're probably right,' she said carefully. 'We don't see eye to eye, do we?'

He put down his coffee-mug and faced her again, his eyes bright with emotion.

'Only on certain issues, Carol. We got on perfectly well until you started house-hunting and suggesting we should move out of the flat and start a family. That house in Cragdale you went to see was far too expensive for us at the time. We simply couldn't afford to stretch our finances with a hefty mortgage.'

Carol rounded on him. 'Euan, that's not true! We could have afforded it. We—'

He leaned forward, every muscle in his body tense. 'I

didn't want us to be short of money just because the house and family couldn't wait until I'd got my fellowship and the prospects of a consultancy. You don't know what it's like, being desperately hard up.'

She saw that his eyes were flashing dangerously and she opened her mouth to try to calm the situation.

'Euan, I think we should stop this discussion before it gets out of hand. I've heard all about your impoverished childhood. You've told me what a hard time your parents had, bringing up five children. You've told me how your father was always working and when he came home he was tired and bad-tempered with you—'

'But that was why I wanted only the best for my own family,' he said, his voice quivering with emotion. 'I wanted to get my fellowship, secure a consultancy and then start the house-hunting and the family part of my life.'

She watched nervously as he pressed both hands to his thighs and leaned further towards her.

'I remember you told me that on Christmas Eve a couple of years ago,' she said. 'On the way home from the hospital I'd driven round to see that beautiful house in Cragdale. I remember feeling so excited about it. It was the sort of house I'd always dreamed we would have. I pulled up at the side of the road on my way home, got out my notebook and worked out our financial situation. We could have afforded it, Euan, and—'

He gave a hoarse laugh. 'There would have been nothing to spare for emergencies, Carol. A bill from the plumber would have upset the whole financial situation. Besides, I didn't want the worry and disruption in the middle of my fellowship studies.'

'So you said when I came home, brimming with excitement. I'd convinced myself I could persuade you into buying the house but—'

'That was just before you walked out on me, wasn't it?'

His voice was a bare whisper.

She clasped her hands together. 'Euan, I had no choice. I could see we were getting nowhere. We were going round in circles and so I told you that if you couldn't change your ideas I was going to leave you and—' She broke off, breathing deeply to calm herself at the awful memory of what had followed.

For several seconds neither of them spoke. It was Euan who broke the silence, his voice husky and full of emotion.

'And I told you I wouldn't stop you going.'

She swallowed hard. 'Yes.'

Her voice faltered as the memory flooded back. She remembered how she hadn't really intended to leave him. She'd thrown out the threat in the hope that he would beg her to stay, tell her he would agree to buy the house if that was what she wanted.

But he'd called her bluff. He'd said if that was how she felt then she'd better go. She remembered that the phone had rung while he'd been speaking. He'd gone to pick it up and she'd heard him saying he would go back to the hospital to see a patient.

He'd picked up his old sheepskin jacket from the sofa where he'd thrown it when he'd got in from a long day in hospital. Her heart had been breaking as she'd watched him shrug into it. He'd seemed to be taking his time. It hadn't been too late to say she didn't want to leave, that she wanted to stay and patch things up.

But he'd gone out of the door, without saying another word—without so much as a backward glance—and she'd been finally convinced he didn't love her any more.

Six months before that fateful Christmas Eve, during

the long hot summer when they were both working long hours and Euan was trying to study in his precious off-duty times, he moved into the spare room. It was a poky little room but he set up a desk in there and a small, narrow bed. And he burned the midnight oil, studying and reading into the small hours.

He told her it was only temporary. He didn't want to disturb her in the night. She needed her sleep. But the cessation of sleeping together had killed the marriage.

So, because their love had been so special in the early days, she decided on that awful Christmas Eve that she couldn't bear to stay on in a dead marriage. Euan's refusal to contemplate buying the Cragdale house had been the nail in the coffin. She couldn't stand any more daily bickering—no fun, no laughter, only long days of work and precious little time to themselves.

She went upstairs, packed a suitcase and wrote Euan a note. She remembered moving about like a robot. She lifted the newly washed clothes out of the washing-machine, straightening out Euan's shirts and putting them on the ironing board. She found herself wondering if she should iron him a shirt. It was Christmas Day the next day and his consultant had asked if he would stand in for him and carve the patients' turkey.

No, she told herself. He would have to manage without her from now on. He didn't want her any more.

It went against all her ideas to harden her heart and simply walk out but she did it. Once outside the house, her thoughts cleared. She knew exactly what she must do to put herself out of her misery.

She went, first of all, to see Janet and asked her to slap an official separation order on Euan. Then she went over to the nurses' home and asked Home Sister for a temporary room. And on Christmas Day she handed in her notice.

When she heard that Euan had asked for an immediate transfer to a London hospital so that he could concentrate on studying for his fellowship she wasn't surprised. It made the four weeks she was working her notice much simpler.

Euan's bleeper was sounding. With an effort she came back to the present.

He was standing now. 'We'd better get back,' he said in an even tone. 'We'll have to finish this conversation later.'

'Euan, we need to make time for a real discussion. I've left a message on Janet's answerphone. She'll be contacting me soon and we need to decide what we're going to do about…'

She paused, drawing in her breath. The word 'divorce' was so final. She'd bandied it about during the last few weeks in a non-emotional way but now, with Euan actually standing beside her…

'You mean the divorce,' he said quietly. 'Yes, we do need to discuss that…at some length. That was why I didn't want to rush into it, why I wanted us to wait until after Christmas before we met up. The last thing I wanted was for you to turn up, insisting we discuss the situation here and now.'

'Not here and now, Euan, some time in the next week when you have a couple of hours off duty,' she said.

He was biting his lip as he looked down at her, his grey eyes tense with a worried expression.

'Two hours? Is that long enough for us to decide what we want to do?' he asked brusquely.

'I thought it might be…before I…'

Before she'd seen Euan again and became swirled up in the vortex of her emotions.

His eyes flickered. 'I think we should definitely talk about this later,' he said firmly.

He opened the door, holding it back so that she could go out in front of him. In the corridor a group of carol-singers was coming towards her. One of them caught sight of Euan and called out to him.

'Mr Maitland, would you like us to sing for you in Accident and Emergency?'

Euan's preoccupied expression relaxed and he smiled at the young, enthusiastic girl.

'Let me check that we haven't got any patients who need peace and quiet. Otherwise, we'd be delighted if you would sing for us. Come into the waiting room while I have a look round.'

Minutes later, the welcome sound of carols was floating through A and E. Carol paused as she put a couple of stitches in an elderly man's hand. Apparently, her patient had dropped a tray of glasses, while handing out drinks to his family, and had then attempted to pick up a jagged piece of glass.

'Does you good—a bit of music, doesn't it, Nurse?' he said, relaxing in the wooden chair. 'Are they taking any requests?'

'Let me finish you off and you can go and ask them yourself. There! How does that feel?'

'Champion, lass! You're a dab hand with a needle and thread. Nearly as good as my missus. You should see the pretty clothes she sews for the grandchildren!'

Carol smiled. 'Would you like a cup of tea, Mr Walker?'

'Not unless you can put a drop of brandy in it.'

'Sorry. I know it's Christmas Eve but—'

'Then I'll be getting off home, love. Thanks for stitching me up. My wife's in the waiting room and we've got a family party to finish back at our house. I wonder if those carol-singers know "Silent Night". I've just time to hear…'

As Carol went into the next cubicle she smiled as she heard "Silent Night" coming from the waiting room. What a nice man Mr Walker was. Rather like Euan's father, very down to earth. Mr Walker was obviously Yorkshire born and bred, whereas Mr Maitland senior was proud of his Scots heritage.

She realised with a pang that she'd missed both her parents-in-law since she'd split from Euan. In some ways they'd helped to replace her own parents who'd died while she was still at school. She'd never thought she'd have missed the bossy Mary Maitland, who'd always been highly critical of her, but she did! Underneath that dour exterior, her mother-in-law only wanted what was best for Euan and Carol. And Thomas Maitland had a heart of gold.

She pushed the thoughts from her mind as she smiled at the young, blonde-haired girl, sitting on her mother's lap.

'Hello, and what's your name?'

'Deirdre,' the little girl whispered shyly.

'And how old are you?'

'Five.' Bright blue eyes stared up at Carol.

'You're a big girl for five. I thought you must be six at least.'

Deirdre preened herself and smiled up at Carol.

'So, would you like to tell me what happened to you?' Carol said gently.

Shyness took over again and the small patient hid her face against her mother's coat, so it was Deirdre's mother who answered.

'Deirdre was playing with one of her new toys. We always let her have a few on Christmas Eve when the grandparents come round. There was this necklace she was making, all like little beads to string and—'

'And I thought it would be nice to have some earrings,' Deirdre suddenly interrupted, sitting up straight and staring earnestly at Carol. 'So I put one of the beads against my ear and it sort of disappeared.'

Deirdre's mother leaned forward. 'She pushed it in her ear, Nurse. I actually saw her do it. I rushed over to stop her but it was gone.'

'And you're sure it didn't drop on the floor?'

'Absolutely sure. It's in there somewhere but I daren't poke around.'

'Well, may I have a look in your ear, Deirdre?'

The little girl pursed her lips and nodded gravely. Her mother gathered her against her ample bosom, an apprehensive expression on her face.

'It's OK,' Carol said gently. 'I'm not going to hurt you...just going to take a quick peep, like this...'

Picking up an auroscope from the trolley, she examined Deirdre's ear. Down at the end of the external auditory canal, clearly outlined against the pearly membrane of the eardrum, she could see a red bead.

'Now, if you could just hold very still for me, Deirdre...'

Carol picked up a pair of curved auditory forceps and gently probed into the ear until she could feel the bead between the ends. Carefully, she withdrew the forceps with the bead clasped between the ends.

'Good girl, Deirdre!' Carol dropped the bead into the palm of her hand and held it out to show the little girl.

'Well, I never!' said Deirdre's mother, clapping her hands together in delight. 'That didn't take long. I had visions of us, having to spend the night here.'

Carol smiled. 'You can go home and have a happy Christmas, but be careful what you do with your beads, Deirdre. Do you want to take this one home with you?'

Deirdre shook her head vigorously. 'No, you can keep

it. I've got lots more. It can be a Christmas present for you. Would you like me to make you a necklace?'

Deirdre's mother was nodding and smiling her agreement.

Carol smiled back. 'That would be lovely but—'

'I'll make it tomorrow and bring it in for you,' Deirdre said happily. 'Happy Christmas!'

'Happy Christmas!' Carol said, carefully rinsing the precious bead under the tap and putting it in her pocket for safe keeping.

The little girl jumped down from her mother's lap and ran to the door of the cubicle, almost bumping into a pair of long, grey-trousered legs.

Carol shot a glance at Euan. The intervening minutes had helped to ease some of the emotional tension between them but she still felt apprehensive.

'Carol, there's a phone call for you,' he said tersely.

'Goodbye, Nurse!' called Deirdre and her mother.

'Goodbye,' Carol said, and then turned back to Euan. 'A phone call for me? It must be Janet. Nobody else knows I'm here.'

'No, it's a man. Mr Nobody is waiting on the phone for you,' Euan said wryly. 'You can take it in my office, if you like. It's probably the quietest spot at the moment. But don't be long. I need some help in the treatment room and everybody else is tied up.'

She hurried into Euan's office and picked up the phone.

'I thought you were planning to rest over Christmas,' said a familiar voice.

'Richard! How did you know where I was?'

'I rang your hotel to wish you a happy Christmas and they told me you'd gone off Florence Nightingaling. What on earth made you want to take a busman's holiday?'

She took a deep breath. Hedonistic Richard wouldn't understand her motives, but she'd better try to explain.

'I felt I owed it to my old training school to help them out in a staff crisis due to a flu epidemic.'

'How very noble!'

She heard the hint of sarcasm in his tone. 'Yes, that's what...somebody else said. Look, did you really just ring to say happy Christmas, Richard? Because we're very busy and I'll have to go back to work so...'

She was aware that Euan had opened the door and was moving over to the drugs cupboard, unlocking it and extracting a phial. Their eyes met as he turned to go out again. She was aware that Richard was talking to her but it was difficult to take in what he was saying with Euan still in the room.

'I was wondering how the divorce plans are going.'

'I don't think my divorce plans are any of your concern, Richard,' she said evenly, desperately aware that Euan had reached the door but had not yet gone out. She held her breath. 'And I really must be going.'

She was silently cursing herself for having talked to Richard at the end-of-cruise party last week. He'd wanted to know why she was trekking north for Christmas, instead of staying in London at the hotel accommodation, provided courtesy of the cruise line, with the rest of the medical team. She'd told him she was going to meet up with her estranged husband and discuss their divorce proceedings.

She had a mental image of Richard, running a manicured hand over his expensively cut, short brown hair, his distinctive features creased into an angry frown.

'I don't want to discuss it over the phone,' she said abruptly. 'Goodbye, Richard.'

'I'll call you again when...' she heard him saying as she put the phone down.

Euan was standing by the door, watching her. 'I couldn't help overhearing,' he said evenly. 'Who's Richard, and why is he so interested in our divorce?'

She took a deep breath. 'Richard is the doctor in charge on the ship I work on.'

Euan moved across the room and perched on the edge of his desk, his face an enigmatic mask.

'Are you having a relationship with this Richard?'

'No, of course not!'

She surprised herself by wanting to assure Euan that there was nothing between her and Richard. Theoretically, since they'd split, she should have felt free to have relationships but she'd never wanted to commit herself. Euan had always been there in her psychological background.

She took a step towards him. He stood up, and she noticed the pulse in his temple, vibrating rapidly. His colour had heightened, his jaw thrusting forward in the familiar pose he'd always adopted when he was feeling annoyed.

Someone knocked on the door.

'We'd better go back,' Carol said quickly.

Fay peeped round the door. 'Oh, sorry. I didn't know—'

'That's OK!' Carol hurried towards her friend. 'We'd just finished.'

'We've got two new admissions,' Fay said. 'Two men involved in a fight. What is it about Christmas Eve that brings out the worst in some people?'

'I've no idea,' Euan said evenly, as he brushed past Carol and went out into the corridor.

'I didn't mean to interrupt you,' Fay said, 'but I'm in the middle of a dressing and senior staff seem thin on the ground at the moment.'

Carol took a deep breath. 'I'm glad you came in when you did. Let's get on with the work.'

The two men were lying on stretchers. Alcohol fumes floated up towards Carol as she leaned over one of the men. Euan was examining the other man.

A distraught young woman was holding onto the side of the trolley.

'He's going to be all right, isn't he, Nurse?'

'Let me take a look while you tell me what happened,' Carol said, cutting away the sleeve of a bloodstained shirt to reveal a long, deep cut from elbow to wrist. Fortunately, the paramedics had applied a tourniquet to the arm to stem the flow of blood.

'Wayne and Darren were drinking in the pub and—'

'Is this Wayne or...?' Carol began as she and the porter moved their patient towards the treatment room.

'No, this is Darren, Nurse,' the young woman explained as she hurried beside them.

Carol noticed that Euan was also heading towards the treatment room with the other patient, a porter pushing the trolley and Staff Nurse Hannah Gregs holding a drip. It was a good thing there were several tables to work on, she thought as the porter helped her to transfer the patient from the trolley to a table.

She glanced at the young woman and smiled reassuringly. 'Now, try not to worry. Darren's going to be all right. Would you like to tell me your name?'

'Tracey,' the young woman said in a wavering voice, still holding tightly to the trolley. 'To be honest, I...'

Euan stepped smartly over and caught Tracey as she fainted. He lifted her up in his arms and placed her gently on the newly vacated trolley. Carol unfolded a blanket and tucked it around Tracey's shoulders.

Darren raised his head from the treatment table and,

screwing up his bloodshot eyes in an effort to focus, said, 'Hey, what's happening to my Tracey?'

'I think it's all been too much for her, Darren,' Carol said. 'We'll have to—'

'She's pregnant,' Darren said, as if that explained everything. 'It wasn't my idea but she insisted she wanted a baby so—'

'You've never treated her properly,' called the second patient, who Carol assumed to be Wayne. His voice was thick with the effects of alcohol and a badly bleeding nose.

'She's my wife,' Darren said.

'If she'd married me—' Wayne began.

'Married you! If she'd married you...'

One of the porters leaned across to restrain Darren, while the other porter held onto the bloody-nosed Wayne. Hannah dropped the kidney dish of swabs with which she was attempting to clean up her patient as she was pushed out of the way.

'Sedation!' Euan said, reaching for a couple of syringes.

Seconds later, Carol and Euan had the situation under control, having succeeded, with the help of the porters, in sedating both their patients.

Carol looked at Euan across the recumbent figure of Darren and breathed a sigh of relief.

'Will you take a look at this wound, Euan? Do we know how it was inflicted? It would be a help if we could find out what actually happened.'

The door opened and, as if on cue, a paramedic hurried across to Euan, handing him a case file.

'Sorry the notes were delayed, Mr Maitland. We had a devil of a time with the pair of them, but the young woman was very helpful. I wrote down what she told me as we came along in the ambulance and then, in the confusion, the notes got lost and—'

'Well, they're here now so let's take a look,' Euan said, scanning the handwritten scrawl, before handing it to Carol.

It appeared that Wayne was Tracey's ex-boyfriend but still continued to go out drinking with Darren after Tracey and Darren were married. When the two men drank too much there would invariably be a fight, but this evening it had got out of hand.

Darren had punched Wayne severely on the face and chest, and Wayne had grabbed the meat knife, with which the pub landlord had been carving the turkey, and had lunged at Darren. Darren had managed to deflect the blade of the knife with his arm but had sustained a deep cut.

'Let's get X-rays of Wayne's nose and chest,' Euan said, signalling to the porter to bring over the portable machine. 'I'll suture this wound, Carol. Looks pretty nasty so we'd better give him some penicillin cover. Will you see to that for me?'

Carol nodded her assent as she went over to the medicine trolley.

Wayne's X-rays showed three broken ribs but the nasal septum was fortunately intact.

'He'll live to fight another day,' Euan said wryly, as he helped Carol to strap up the broken ribs.

'Finish this off and I'll get a cup of tea for Tracy,' Carol said, straightening. 'I've made her comfortable on one of the examination couches and told her you'll take a look at her as soon as you're free.'

'How far on is she?' Euan asked, fixing a final clip on the end of the adhesive strip.

'She thinks about three months.' Carol hesitated. 'Would you like a cup of tea, by any chance?'

He raised his eyes to hers. 'Now when have I ever said no? To a cup of tea,' he added, with the sort of smile that always used to tear at her heartstrings and was having an emotionally devastating effect on her now.

She turned away. 'Milk, no sugar?'

She hated the way her voice cracked when she was feeling emotional. She was only making Euan a cup of tea, for heaven's sake! No need to go all nostalgic!

But as she went over to the little side room she couldn't help recalling how they'd always had a cup of tea...afterwards. It had always been Euan who'd got out of bed to make it. Sometimes, she'd started to get out first but he had put out a restraining hand and told her that he'd wanted her to stay right where she was so that...

She turned on the cold tap and while she filled the kettle she told herself to stop harking back to the past. Those idyllic days were all gone. It was impossible to turn back the clock. She had to go forward to whatever the future held.

'Are you making that for me, Nurse?'

Tracey was standing in the doorway, one hand smoothing down her long, blonde hair. 'I feel much better now so I thought I'd see how Darren and Wayne are getting on. The nurses and porters have just taken them up to the wards so—'

'Sit down here, Tracey, and drink a cup of tea,' Carol said gently. 'You need to take care of yourself. Don't worry about the men—they're going to be OK.'

'It was the same last Christmas Eve,' Tracey said as she sipped her tea. 'The pair of them went out and got legless. Then the fighting started and we finished up in here, Darren with a cut eye and Wayne with a broken jaw. I don't know what it is about Christmas Eve.'

Carol looked up and saw that Euan was coming

through the open door. He sat down next to Tracey.
Carol reached for the teapot and handed him a cup of
tea.

'Yes, what is it about Christmas Eve that brings out
the worst in some people?' he said in a barely audible
voice. He took a sip of tea and placed his cup on the
small table.

Carol tensed. 'Is it because Christmas is such a special
time we feel we have to put everything to rights, sort
out all our problems before the big day?'

Tracey gave a weary smile. 'It might be. In my experience it's mainly due to the drink.'

Euan gave a wry smile as his eyes caught Carol's.
'We didn't have the excuse of alcohol, did we?'

Tracey looked quizzically from one to the other.

Carol quickly took charge of the situation. 'Have you
made the arrangements for Tracey to be checked over,
Euan?'

'Yes.' He gave his worried-looking patient a reassuring smile. 'I've arranged for you to have a bed on the
obstetrics ward tonight, Tracey, and one of the obstetri-
cians will take a look at you.'

'But I'm fine! It was all the excitement and everything. I'll go up and see Darren now and then I'll go
home, Doctor. Just tell me which ward he's on. It's all
signposted and, anyway, I've been here so many times
I won't get lost.'

'Darren's on Male Surgical and Wayne's on Male
Orthopaedic,' Euan said, 'but I really think…'

'How would you get home, Tracey?' Carol asked
gently.

Tracey looked surprised. 'On the bus, of course.'

'Is there anyone at home to be with you?' Euan said.

'No, we live on our own, Darren and me.'

'I really think you should stay the night, Tracey, and

be looked after…for the sake of your baby,' Euan added firmly.

The young woman gave a resigned smile. 'OK.' She glanced from Euan to Carol. 'Thanks, you've been great. If I don't see you in the morning, Happy Christmas!'

Neither of them spoke for a few seconds after Tracey had gone. It seemed strangely quiet.

'Another calm before another storm,' Carol said, finding the silence too much to handle, sitting as close as she was to Euan.

She moved to stand up but he put out a restraining hand.

'Don't go. Let's have a couple of minutes to ourselves. We do need to talk, you know.'

She felt the butterflies surface again in her stomach but she remained seated.

'As I was saying just now, it wasn't drink that brought out the worst in us on that Christmas Eve,' he said. 'As I recall, our feet hadn't touched the ground all day so neither of us had had the time to visit the off-licence and there wasn't a drop of anything remotely festive in the house.'

Carol gave a wry smile as she leaned back.

'There was that bottle of orange juice that your mother sent when she heard I'd had flu.'

Euan laughed and as the sound echoed out across the empty treatment room Carol thought how much she'd missed Euan's laughter. In the early days of their marriage they'd laughed such a lot. It had only been in the last six months that—

'I was planning to go to the off-licence and take out a mortgage on a bottle of champagne when—' Euan stopped in mid-sentence and turned to face her.

She blinked as she saw the raw pain in his eyes.

'You mean when I told you I'd seen a house I wanted us to buy...and we started arguing again and—'

She broke off, realising that if she continued there was a real danger she might start crying. The whole awful episode had been more than she could stand at the time, and just talking about it now made it all the worse.

She was faintly aware that Euan was reaching out towards her with both hands. She tensed but remained quite still, mesmerised by the expression of deeply caring emotion in his eyes.

His sensitive fingers touched her face and slid gently down either side until he was holding the back of her neck. Slowly, oh, so slowly, he pulled her face towards him. She saw his lips hovering near hers. She felt she should pull herself away and yet she allowed the momentum to continue.

It was like being part of a slow-motion film. She felt powerless to resist the magnetism of his lips. How many times had she drowned herself in them?

There was only a narrow gap separating their lips now. The reasoning part of her brain told her to resist but her treacherous heart urged her to capitulate, to go with the flow.

She felt the first pressure of his skin and then the full-bodied warmth that she remembered so well. She gave an audible sigh of excitement as he pulled her against him.

The phone started ringing and its shrill, clamorous call brought her back to her senses. She realised with a pang of dismay that for several seconds she'd been completely out of control. She'd kissed Euan in a way that could only mean reconciliation. And until they'd sorted out their differences in a logical way she shouldn't let her nostalgic emotions cloud the issue and affect her judgement.

She pulled herself away, her hand automatically checking that the false hairpiece was still in place.

'That makes you look different, sort of more sophisticated. I'm not sure…' Euan said, as he reached out to touch the top of her head with one hand while the other still lingered on her shoulder.

With a visible effort he pulled himself to his feet and went over to answer the phone.

She couldn't help but admit that he looked undeniably boyish and handsome, his face relaxed and his voice carefree as he answered the call. Just like the first months of their marriage when neither of them had felt they had a care in the world simply because they had each other.

'Hello!'

She watched as he listened, trying desperately to calm her turbulent emotions. It was only a kiss, a little kiss…but she'd been desperately moved by it. After two years of trying to convince herself that it was all over between them…

'It's for you, Carol. Janet Manson, your solicitor. Says you left a message on her answerphone. I presume this is concerning the divorce.'

His voice was cold. He looked away as he handed her the phone. She felt the emotional temperature plummet below freezing as she took the phone from his outstretched hand.

CHAPTER THREE

CAROL could feel her spirits sinking as she watched
Euan leave the room without a backward glance. With
an awful feeling of apprehension, she spoke into the receiver.

'Hello, Janet.'

'Carol! I got your message, asking me to call you at
the hotel, and they told me you were working at the
hospital. It's very noble of you to give up your
Christmas Eve!'

How many more people were going to tell her how
noble she was?

She could hear the sound of music and chattering in
the background at Janet's house, and had a sudden mental image of her blonde, extrovert, always-socially-in-
demand school chum, surrounded by friends and family,
trying to clear her answerphone before Christmas Day
with typical efficiency.

'Thanks for returning my call, Janet. I didn't intend
you to have to call me back on Christmas Eve. I simply
wanted to make contact and fix a time when we could
get together after Christmas. You must be rushed off
your feet so—'

'Oh, that's OK, Carol. Just a few people in for a buffet
supper. If I'd known you were here I would have invited
you along. We're off to Wales tomorrow at the crack of
sparrows to stay with Hugh's parents for a week so I'm
clearing the messages. You said you wanted my professional advice so fire away.'

In the background, Carol could hear someone, playing

the piano, and she remembered that Hugh, Janet's husband, who'd been in the form above them at school, had studied at the Royal College of Music, before teaching at the local grammar school. Several voices were already joining in as he began to play 'In the Bleak Midwinter'.

She was beginning to feel decidedly bleak herself! Since leaving that message for Janet this afternoon, circumstances had changed considerably.

No, they haven't! she reminded herself firmly. Just because you've actually seen Euan again and he didn't jump down your throat every time you opened your mouth and you felt a few twinges of nostalgia, creeping down your spine...

She swallowed. 'Janet, I've seen Euan this evening but we haven't had time for a proper discussion. We're going to meet up during Christmas week and sort out how we feel about a divorce. It's all rather complicated, as you can imagine. We haven't seen each other for two years and Euan doesn't want to be rushed into a decision. Perhaps we could meet you in a few days' time when we've had time to assess the situation.'

She paused for breath. Over the phone she could hear Christmas music. 'Snow had fallen, snow on snow...' she heard as she waited for a reply.

'I must admit I'd always hoped you two would get back together again. In fact, knowing that Euan was back in Moortown, it crossed my mind that—'

'It's not easy, Janet, to pretend this separation never happened. Meeting up for a few hours isn't like living together.'

Carol surprised herself at the vehemence with which she pronounced these words. She knew she was trying to quell the disturbing emotions that were churning inside her.

'Well, in that case, I'll be totally professional,' came

Janet's clipped tones over the phone. 'How does Euan feel about this?'

'I'm not sure. I assumed, before I saw him this evening, that, having walked out and slapped the two-year separation order on him—'

She broke off as she tried to work out what it was she was trying to say. Had Euan's kiss addled her brain so that she could no longer think straight?

'Was that Euan who answered the phone just now, Carol?' Janet asked in her totally professional voice.

'Yes, we're working together but—'

'Look, maybe we'd better leave this till I get back from Wales,' Janet said in a diplomatically bland tone. 'How long are you going to be in Moortown?'

'A week and then I sail from Southampton around the world again. I thought we could—'

'In that case, the best thing is if I pop round and see you this evening,' Janet said briskly, as if sensing the ambivalence of Carol's intentions. 'I'm away all next week. We'll just have a friendly chat so that I can explain the implications of what a divorce would entail if you decide to go ahead with it.'

Carol felt a wave of something akin to panic sweep over her. Events were moving too quickly. She needed time to reassess the situation.

'Janet, I can't drag you out on Christmas Eve!'

The unwelcome butterflies were doing a war dance in her stomach. Why did Janet have to be so super-efficient?

'Yes, you can.' The clipped tones came back loud, clear and no-nonsense. 'What are friends for? When do you get a break?'

Carol swallowed hard. 'I've got an hour from midnight but—'

'Then I'll see you during your break. Hugh can clear

away the mess and finish packing while I'm out. Which department are you in?'

'Accident and Emergency, but I'll be in the medical staff dining room for part of the time unless we have a staffing problem—talking of which, I really must get back to work. Thanks a lot, Janet.'

As she put the phone down she could hear Janet's guests, doing an impromptu rendition of the 'Hallelujah Chorus', which helped to raise her spirits a little, but as she hurried out of the treatment room back into the main receiving area she felt as if she'd just arranged to commit some awful crime.

How could she even contemplate dealing the final blow to her relationship with Euan?

Fay was hurrying towards her. 'Are you all right, Carol? You look as if you've seen a ghost.'

She forced herself to smile. 'I think maybe I have!' She took a deep breath to steady her nerves. 'I'm fine! What would you like me to do next?'

'There's a newly admitted child in cubicle one. Euan's with him at the moment. I'll be dressing a leg wound in the treatment room if you need me.'

Euan looked up as she went into the cubicle. His eyes held a neutral expression and his stance was totally professional. They'd returned to being simply medical colleagues.

Quietly he filled her in on the details of the case. Their patient, Adam Grayson, three years old, had been brought in by the parents because he had a high temperature, he'd been sick and they'd noticed spots on his abdomen. Adam's mother was, understandably, looking very worried. Her husband had gone out for a smoke to calm his nerves.

Adam's mother put a hand on Carol's arm and confided, 'What we're worrying about is whether Adam's got meningitis. You hear such a lot about it in the papers and on the telly. I reckon you can't be too careful. He's been really sick all day, Nurse, and he's so hot. I gave him some Calpol but it hasn't worked like it usually does.'

Carol glanced at the temperature chart. A hundred and three degrees Fahrenheit. She looked down at the sick child whose fair hair was plastered against his head, sucking his thumb and clutching a battered teddy bear as he whimpered quietly.

'Poor little Adam!' she said softly, reaching down to pull back the thin cotton of his Power Rangers T-shirt. She stroked the teddy bear. 'And who's this?'

'Teddy,' came the muffled reply as Adam stopped sucking for a couple of seconds and looked up at Carol.

'He's a lovely bear,' she said, as she noted the scattering of purpuric spots on Adam's skin. Gently, she put her fingers on a small section and stretched the skin. The spots didn't disappear as she'd hoped they would.

She looked at Euan, who nodded to indicate that he'd already done that test. If the spots had disappeared on stretching they could have discounted meningitis. As it was, they would have to do further tests.

'We're going to take Adam to the treatment room to do a little test, Mrs Grayson,' Euan said gently. 'We'll take some of the fluid from his spinal canal and see if we can identify the problem. Do you want to come with us?'

Adam's mother shook her head. 'No, I think I'd only get in the way.' She lowered her voice. 'I'm a bit squeamish, Doctor.' Raising her voice again, she said, 'Adam will be better off with the nice doctor and the kind nurse, won't you, Adam?'

The little boy didn't reply as he curled himself up in a ball and closed his eyes.

'The high temperature is making him very drowsy,' Carol said. 'We'll take good care of him. Why don't you go and join your husband for a coffee?'

'And a cigarette!' Mrs Grayson said. 'I stopped smoking three months ago but I think I'll have a couple to see me through. It's times like this when I go all to pieces and it's been such a terrible day!'

Euan put out his hand and patted Mrs Grayson's shoulder. 'Don't worry. We'll take good care of Adam.

'The porters are all busy,' Euan said briskly, as soon as Mrs Grayson had left them alone with Adam. 'I'll push the trolley.'

He lifted Adam from the examination couch. Out in the corridor Carol could see Phil Morton, their dark-haired senior registrar, and a couple of nurses, trying to persuade a man with a bandage round his head to sit down in a wheelchair.

'There's nothing wrong with me... I want to go home. I want to go home,' the man was saying in a thick, almost indecipherable voice.

Euan hurried over to help Phil.

'Concussion,' Phil said in a strained voice. 'We'll have to keep him in overnight. We can't let him go in this state.'

Euan started to reason with the distraught patient. Hearing the noise, little Adam began to cry so Carol hurriedly pushed the trolley towards the treatment room.

She'd managed to placate her little patient and had set out the instruments for a lumbar puncture by the time Euan joined her again.

She looked up. 'How's the concussion patient?'

Euan breathed a sigh of relief. 'They've taken him up to Male Medical.'

He smiled down at Adam. 'Now, little man, let's have

a look at you, shall we? Just roll over on your side for me…that's good… If you can hold him there, Carol…'

Swiftly Euan scrubbed his hands while Carol fixed sterile towels round the little boy's back. Euan returned to inject a local anaesthetic into the spot from where he would withdraw the fluid.

'Good boy, Adam!' Carol said, squeezing her small patient's hand.

Blue, trusting eyes stared up at her as Adam continued to suck his thumb and hold tightly to his beloved Teddy.

'Teddy's thirsty,' Adam said solemnly.

'And are you thirsty?' Carol asked, holding Adam still whilst Euan inserted a needle between the third and fourth lumbar vertebrae.

Good! Adam hadn't noticed what Euan was doing so he obviously felt no pain.

'Yes, I'd like a drink,' Adam said.

'Well, I'll get you one just as soon as Doctor has finished looking at your back. Just hold still for a little while…'

She saw Euan withdrawing some cerebrospinal fluid into a large syringe. She handed him a sterile test tube.

'We'll get that off to the lab as soon as possible,' Euan said, sealing up the package and handing it to Carol.

He smiled down at Adam. 'All right, little man. You can have that drink now.'

'What a good boy you've been!' Carol said, as she held a glass of water to Adam's lips.

'Now it's Teddy's turn,' Adam said, wiping his mouth with the back of his hand.

Carefully, Carol held the glass to Teddy's mouth. Euan made suitable slurping noises and Adam laughed.

'I told you Teddy was thirsty.' The little boy giggled. 'Has he got any spots?'

'I'd better take a look,' Euan said solemnly, stretching

the scant, battered fur with his fingers. 'He seems all right but I'll check him out later when he's had a rest in the ward bed with you. How's Teddy's chest, I wonder?'

Euan put his stethoscope on Teddy's chest and pretended to listen. 'Now it's your turn, Adam...'

Carol turned away and brushed a hand over her eyes. Euan would make a wonderful father.

She went over to the phone and called the path lab, asking for someone to collect the precious sample for analysis as soon as possible. Then she called Paediatrics and asked them to admit Adam to a side ward to be nursed under special conditions because of the possibility that meningitis might be the diagnosis.

She went over to the treatment table and helped Euan to give Adam some penicillin.

'Until we've isolated the organism that's causing this fever we'd better get some antibiotics working,' he said quietly.

Carol reached down and felt the back of Adam's neck. 'There's still no retraction, Euan,' she said, feeling relieved that Adam wasn't lying with his head thrust backward in the stiff pose so typical of meningitis patients.

Euan nodded. 'Let's hope our provisional diagnosis is incorrect,' he said softly, as he lifted Adam and Teddy back onto the trolley.

'Will Mummy and Daddy come and see me in the new bed?' Adam asked in a small voice.

Carol smiled down at him. 'Yes, I'll send them along very soon.'

The swing doors opened and a nurse from Paediatrics arrived with a porter.

'Goodbye, Adam!' Euan said, holding open the door for the trolley to go through.

Carol moved to follow them out into the corridor but Euan put out a restraining hand.

'Don't go, Carol. We need to talk.'

The swing doors shut again. Carol felt a shiver of apprehension run down her spine.

'When you spoke to Janet on the phone did you tell her we needed more time to discuss our situation?'

Carol hesitated. 'I said we were going to have an in-depth discussion some time during the next few days. She suggested she came over this evening for a preliminary chat and—'

'This evening?'

'She's going away until after New Year so she simply wants to explain the implications of a divorce and—'

'I would have thought the implications of a divorce were obvious,' he said tersely, 'but I suppose it won't do any harm to have a third party, giving us her opinions.'

Carol felt a certain sense of relief. 'Then you don't mind seeing Janet with me?'

'Well, let's say, as I'm so involved in this, I need to be there when you're discussing my whole future.'

'Janet's agreed to come to the staff dining room between midnight and one so...'

'I'll be there. Although it's probably better if we take her to my office. And, Carol...'

He put out both his hands to touch the sides of her sleeves. She looked up at him, her heart beating so wildly she was sure he would hear.

'No more recriminations, OK? Let's try to remain objective in our discussion.'

His eyes were enigmatic as he looked down at her. He seemed to be experiencing none of the wild emotions that were churning inside her. This was what she wanted...wasn't it?

'I agree. No more recriminations…on either side,' she said blandly.

Euan was holding open the door, his eyes hooded with a veiled expression.

She forced herself to concentrate wholeheartedly on the patients who needed her help and medical expertise for the rest of the evening. Just before midnight, as she was stitching a hand wound on a young man, Fay came into the treatment room.

'You can go off duty when you've finished that,' Fay said. 'It's easing off in the reception area. I'll go for dinner at one when you get back.'

Carol trimmed the final stitch with her scissors and looked up at Fay.

'Janet's coming to see me between twelve and one,' she said quietly. She glanced down at her patient. 'Would you like to stand up now, Paul? If you feel OK you can—'

'Thanks, Nurse.' The young man shot out through the door.

Fay grinned. 'Three of Paul's mates are waiting for him in Reception. They're anxious to rejoin their Christmas party.'

'Why do people always try to pick up broken bottles with their bare hands?' Carol said.

'Beats me! So Janet's coming here? Would you like to use my office?'

'That's very kind of you, Fay, but…we're going to use Euan's.'

'So he's agreed to see Janet about divorce proceedings?'

'Yes.'

'And that's what you both want?'

'Yes.'

Fay turned away. 'Well, you could have fooled me!'

'Fay, don't make it any harder than it is to—'

'Exactly!' Fay rounded on Carol, her eyes flashing. 'If you ask me, you both need your heads examining!'

Carol swallowed. 'I've set the wheels in motion and we—'

'Then put the brakes on, for heaven's sake! It's not too late! It's never too late to—'

Fay broke off as the swing door opened. Euan stood with one hand on the door, waiting for Fay to finish her sentence.

'Never too late for what, Fay?' he prompted.

Fay drew in her breath. 'Carol's just been telling me that Janet is coming to discuss your divorce. If you want my opinion—'

'Thank you, Fay, we don't,' Euan said quickly. 'This is between Carol and me.'

'Fine!' Fay said in a forced, pseudo-light-hearted tone. 'I'll say no more about it.'

At the door, she turned back. 'You haven't forgotten you're supposed to be carving the staff turkey at midnight, have you, Euan? If you'd like me to ask Phil Morton to do it so you have more time for consultation with Janet, I—'

'Of course I haven't forgotten. The highlight of my Christmas Eve,' he added, jokingly. 'I wouldn't dream of missing it.'

'Well, you'd better get a move on,' Fay said, glancing up at the large round wall clock where the hands were both pointing to the twelve.

'A double celebration,' Euan said. 'Christmas morning and Carol's birthday, all on the same day.'

'I'd forgotten! Happy Birthday, Carol!' Fay said. 'I'd better get back.'

'Happy Birthday!' Euan said in a calm voice as soon

as they were alone. 'And I really mean it,' he added, his eyes searching her face for a reaction.

She looked up at him as he held open the door but his eyes gave nothing away.

'We'd better move if I'm to carve that turkey,' he said.

She heard the hint of huskiness in his voice and something about the way he looked away told her that he wasn't taking this divorce business as calmly as he tried to make out.

They walked along the corridor, side by side, their hands almost, but not quite, touching. As Euan pushed open the staff dining room door they were immediately drawn into the carnival atmosphere of the Christmas celebrations.

'Over here, Mr Maitland!' called the chef, who was placing an enormous turkey on the top table.

Paper streamers hung from the ceiling and a large tree, decorated with silver tinsel and shiny, coloured balls, glistened in the corner of the room. For a moment Carol stood rooted to the spot, overwhelmed by the sense of nostalgia which threatened to engulf her as vivid memories of previous Christmases in this dining room returned to haunt her.

It had been in the middle of one particularly busy Christmas Eve that Euan had proposed to her, here in this very room, over by the Christmas tree.

She did a rapid calculation. Yes, it must have been four years ago. It seemed like a lifetime away. It had been the Christmas Eve staff lunch. She was Sister of Female Surgical and Euan was a senior surgical registrar. They'd only known each other three months but it had been obvious to Carol, right from the start, that this was the only man she'd ever love.

Oh, she'd had several boyfriends, some short term,

some longer, but none of them had touched her heart like Euan had done. She remembered how he'd come to sit next to her at the table and they'd laughed and joked their way through the prawn cocktail. Then, in the gap between the first and second courses he'd said there was a present for her on the tree.

He'd pulled back her chair and put his hand under her arm and then loosely around her waist as she'd walked with him to the tree. And then he'd pointed to a medium-sized package, wrapped in gold paper. She'd unwrapped it, aware that the dining room had become unusually quiet. Inside had been a pair of earrings. She remembered taking them out of the tissue paper and enthusing over them, secretly wishing it had been what she'd hoped for.

She'd felt his hand on her arm and seen that he'd been slipping the other hand into his pocket to bring out another smaller, brown leather box. This one hadn't been wrapped. Her heart had stood still as she'd looked at it. His fingers had stretched out towards her and she'd taken the box from him and opened it, trying to stifle her gasp of happiness as she'd stared down at the gold and diamond solitaire ring.

She'd looked up at him and his eyes had pleaded with her.

'Will you marry me, Carol?' he said quietly, in that husky, emotional tone which always made her weak at the knees.

She was too full for words. Initially she nodded and then, as he moved to put the ring on her finger, she found enough voice to whisper, 'Yes.'

And the whole dining room cheered and shouted their congratulations, crowding round to see the ring and wish them every happiness…

Euan's voice broke through her thoughts. 'Come and help me, Carol.'

He was taking hold of her hand, leading her along to the top table. She felt as if she'd been propelled back in time…but, no, this was real, this was happening now. Euan's fingers over hers meant nothing—to him. But to her…

They reached the top table, and the chef was smiling at them.

'And Mrs Maitland as well. Lovely to see you again!'

A chair was pulled out for her. She sat down and looked around the crowded room. Familiar faces swam before her eyes and she forced herself to smile. A couple of nurses brought a surgical gown and mask and began the ceremonial robing up of the surgeon.

She looked up and saw that Euan was really entering into the spirit of the occasion as he allowed himself to be dressed. Holding the knife and sharpener above the turkey, he flashed the steel blades and everybody cheered. He laid the gastronomic instruments on the table and waited for the cheering to stop, before pronouncing the important words, 'Scalpel, Sister!'

Carol watched as chestnut-haired Theatre Sister Peggy Rawson, who was sitting on the other side of Euan, handed him the requisite knife. He began to carve and the cheers broke out again.

Vegetables were handed round, gravy was poured and the Christmas feast began. Looking round the room, she felt as if she'd never been away.

'I hope you didn't mind me dragging you up here,' Euan said quietly. 'I thought people would be less likely to overwhelm you with questions if you were at the top table.'

She smiled. 'I think you're probably right.'

Glancing along their table at the young theatre staff

who were tucking in to their meal, she didn't recognise anybody. They'd all started working here after she'd left so there was nobody here who would start asking embarrassing questions.

'I've saved this for you,' Euan said, putting the turkey wishbone on the side of her plate.

For an instant she stared at him, without replying. Ever since their first Christmas together, when he'd discovered she loved to pull the wishbone, he'd always saved it for her. But tonight was different. They would soon be discussing their divorce and—

She checked her reaction as she saw the tender expression in his eyes. It seemed as if, in facing up to the possibility of a divorce, they'd both rid themselves of the emotional baggage of the past. All the recriminations and misunderstandings could be swept away and they could be friends again.

He picked up the wishbone from her plate and held it out towards her. She took hold of the end he was offering her. They both pulled. The bones snapped and Carol was left with the bigger portion, which gave her the right to make the magic wish.

She smiled. 'I wonder why that always happens when we do this? You fixed it so I would win again, didn't you?'

He laughed. 'Would I? Knowing how much you enjoy making the magic wish? Well, go on, then…get wishing.'

She closed her eyes and for an instant she went back to their first Christmas together. She remembered exactly what she'd wished for. Tonight was totally different. She had to be objective, she had to be realistic…

She opened her eyes.

'Are you going to tell me what you wished for,

Carol?' His voice was jocular but the expression in his eyes was deadly serious as he leaned towards her.

'Certainly not!' she said, trying desperately to enter into the carnival atmosphere as she gave him a mock reprimand. 'And don't even think about guessing.'

He laughed again and the haunting sound sent shivers down her spine. It was good to be friends again.

She glanced sideways at Euan as he turned to speak to Peggy, and realised that tonight had been like meeting him again for the first time. She felt the same tremendous attraction towards him that she'd felt on that first occasion when he'd walked onto her ward as the new senior surgical registrar.

It had been the first of September, four years and three months ago. She remembered she'd had a good, auspicious start to the morning. Coming out of her room in the nurses' home, she'd remembered to greet the first person she'd spoken to with the words, 'White rabbits!'

Being the first of the month, it was good luck. She always told herself she wasn't really superstitious, but right from childhood she'd been pleased if she'd remembered to say, 'White rabbits!' on the first of the month and sorry if she forgot. So she'd felt that something exciting was going to happen that day.

She remembered how she'd taken the report from Night Sister and started the medicine round with one of her trainee staff nurses.

Halfway down the ward she glanced up to see the ward doors opening. Mr Thorpe, the grey-haired, soon-to-be-retired surgical consultant appeared, complete with surgical staff entourage. She recognised the two housemen, Mr Thorpe's secretary and the junior registrar—but there was one man she'd never seen before.

He was tall, dark and, to complete the picture—even though it sounded corny—he was also very handsome.

His white coat hung loosely over a grey pinstriped suit. He looked lean and athletic, and the twinkle in his expressive eyes as she joined the group told her that he would be good fun to be with.

And she knew in that instant that this was the man she'd been waiting for. She felt the spark that flashed between them and she remembered how, on their wedding night, Euan had told her he'd felt exactly the same. It was as if a current of electricity had passed between them...

She was brought back to the present when, glancing across the room, she suddenly saw Janet, in a chic, expensive-looking black suit, standing in the open doorway. How appropriate that her solicitor friend should be wearing black when they were about to start discussing the possibility of ending their marriage.

Carol raised her hand and signalled that she would join her.

'Euan, Janet's here,' she said quietly.

'Afraid we've got to go,' Euan told Peggy.

'Would you like me to save you both some pudding?' the theatre sister asked, her smiling eyes showing how anxious she was to please.

'Not for me,' Carol said quickly. 'I don't think I'll have time.'

Plates were being cleared and the chef had already appeared with a large Christmas pudding, flaming in brandy. Euan made his apologies, saying he would return later if he could.

'You don't do things by halves in this hospital,' Janet said, as the three of them walked down the corridor towards Euan's office. 'I'd no idea all this was going on in the middle of the night.'

Euan smiled. 'It's one of the reasons why the staff

don't find it too hard to work on Christmas Eve. And the ones without families positively vie with each other to work over Christmas. You know, the single and divorced ones without children.'

'Understandable, really,' Janet said in a conversational tone.

Carol remained silent as the irony of the situation forced itself upon her. Was that another reason why she'd volunteered to work tonight—because she hadn't wanted to spend Christmas alone in the hotel?

She'd carefully avoided contacting her only remaining relatives in the area, knowing that her mother's cousin, Brenda, and her husband, Colin, with whom she'd lived after her parents died, would have insisted she stayed with them if they'd known she was in Moortown. But they would have asked too many questions and it would have been emotionally exhausting.

They'd now reached Euan's room. Once inside, he pulled up a couple of chairs for Carol and himself, and invited Janet to sit in his place behind the desk.

'You need somewhere to unload your briefcase and laptop so you'll be more comfortable there,' he told her.

'Thanks.' Janet carefully placed her leather gloves inside her handbag, fixed the laptop computer in front of her and looked across the desk at Carol.

'You've been apart for two years, haven't you?' she asked in a neutral voice.

Carol nodded. 'That's correct.'

'And, remind me, how long had you been married before you split?'

'Eighteen months,' Euan said evenly. 'The first year was fine. It was the last six months that were…difficult.'

'What was the reason you split up?'

Looking at Janet, Carol could see why she had a reputation for being good at her job. She was able to main-

tain total professionalism in spite of the fact that they
were old school chums.

'We were having arguments all the time and—'

'Arguments about what?'

'Well…' Carol glanced at Euan.

'Anything and everything, but the main bone of contention was that Carol wanted to buy a house, move out
of the flat and start a family,' Euan said. 'I wanted to
wait until after I'd got my fellowship and moved up the
career ladder, for obvious reasons, mostly financial.'

Carol resisted the temptation to argue at this point.

'Family finances are very important,' Janet said, her
shrewd eyes sweeping from Euan to Carol. 'Failure to
keep within the agreed budget often—'

'But Euan and I could never agree on a budget,' Carol
broke in. 'I thought he was always too cautious about
spending and—'

She broke off in embarrassment. Euan was looking at
her with a wry expression.

'Yes, I do have a different way of looking at things
to you, Carol. I think you're too impulsive. I like to
weigh up a situation, before jumping in with both feet.'

'So, has anything changed in these two years of separation?' asked Janet briskly. 'I remember how upset
Carol was when she came to see me on that Christmas
Eve. She was adamant that she wanted to end the marriage.'

Euan cleared his throat. 'In my experience, basic per-
sonalities never change. Carol and I would have to agree
to differ…'

Carol could feel her heart beginning to thump loudly
as she listened to Euan.

'Because I don't think one person should ever try to
change another. On the other hand, if circumstances
change so that the financial constraints have eased…'

He spread his hands out in front of him, frowning as he seemed to search for the right words to express himself.

'What you're trying to say,' put in Janet helpfully, 'is that you need to reassess the situation, before going ahead with a divorce.'

'Exactly!' Euan said. 'Which was why I didn't want to be rushed into a discussion over Christmas when I'm starting a new job.'

'Let me put all this on hold until the New Year,' Janet said evenly. 'When you've talked everything through you can contact me and let me know if you've decided to go ahead with the divorce or not.'

Euan was nodding as he looked at Carol enquiringly.

'Yes, I think we should take our time,' she agreed.

'Well, then, let me just put down a few more details,' Janet said. 'This is just so that if you do decide to go ahead with the divorce in the New Year I'll have all the facts organised.'

She was staring at the screen on her laptop as she began to tap away on the keys. Every now and then she would ask a question, before returning to her computer.

Carol felt as if she were in a dream...correction, a nightmare! This couldn't be happening to her...but it was. And it was a nightmare of her own making.

She stared up at the ceiling as she tried to compose her thoughts. A spider was making its way carefully across the white plaster, scurrying towards the far corner of the room. It looked frightened, trapped in this room and unable to escape. She knew exactly how it must be feeling.

But Fay had said it was never too late. She looked across at Euan but he avoided her glance. His answers to Janet's questions were precise and totally devoid of emotion. It was as if they were considering selling a house, not a marriage.

Janet closed down her laptop and rose, extending her hand across the desk.

'I can get on with this while I'm in Wales,' she said in a bland, professional tone. 'I always get bored after the first day of family reunions. It will be good to have an excuse to hide away and do some work. Thank goodness for modern technology. I don't know how I'd live without my fax and my computer and my mobile phone.'

Euan was shaking Janet's hand. For an instant Carol thought her friend was going to lose her professional cool as she put a gloved hand on each of their arms. There was a look of concern as she studied the pair of them.

'I must say you're the most amicable couple I've ever met, who were discussing divorce. It's almost a surprise to me that— Goodness, is that the time? Hugh will think I've run away with Father Christmas.'

She paused by the door, once more the impartial solicitor.

'I nearly forgot... Happy Birthday, Carol!'

Carol forced a smile. 'Thanks!'

Janet hovered in the doorway. 'If there's anything further you want to ask me, give me a call in the morning. We plan to leave as early as possible but I don't expect it will be much before nine. Bye.'

'What a relief to get all those questions out of the way!' Euan said as the door closed. 'But, I must admit, I thought it would take much longer. Organising a divorce seems quicker than getting married, doesn't it?'

'I can't remember much about the actual wedding day,' Carol said quietly. 'It all passed in a bit of a haze.'

He took a step towards her. 'I know what you mean. I felt totally spaced out myself...but I do remember that you looked wonderful.'

She held her breath as he put out his hand and touched

her face, gently running his fingers over her skin. 'And when you pulled back your veil I remember thinking I'd never seen you look so lovely. Your eyes were—'

'Euan, I don't think we should get into any more nostalgia,' she said, turning her head and moving away so that he wouldn't see the tears that threatened to escape down her cheek.

'Why not?' He put his hands on her shoulders and gently turned her to face him. 'I'll never regret a moment of our first year together.'

She swallowed hard, willing her eyes to remain dry. 'Neither will I,' she said.

'Remember our first Christmas when we deliberated over whether we could afford a real Christmas tree, and—?'

'And you went out to the open-air market on Christmas Eve when they were selling them off cheap and you got the biggest one you could find, and—'

'And it was so big I had to chop the top off before—' He stopped in mid-sentence.

His grey eyes held an expression of real tenderness as he bent his head towards her.

She knew he was going to kiss her and she stood stock still, anticipating the heady moment—wanting the feel of his lips more than anything in the world. And when the expected kiss materialised she gave a deep inward sigh.

Seconds later he was pulling away.

'Sealed with a loving kiss,' he said huskily. 'I remember writing that on my first love letter when I was about twelve. I'm not sure whether it's appropriate to seal a divorce discussion with a kiss.'

He placed a finger under her chin and tilted her face upwards towards him. His eyes remained tender, his mouth seductively poised above her.

'What are you thinking, Carol?'

'I'm thinking about how different we both are and whether—'

'Whether we could ever sink our differences?'

She swallowed. 'Something like that. What did you mean when you said that circumstances change?'

'I was talking about the fact that I've actually got my fellowship now, secured my post as a consultant and my salary has improved considerably.'

His eyes flickered as he looked down at her. She waited, realising that she wanted him to be more explicit, but when he said nothing she said, 'So some of the obstacles have been removed, haven't they?'

He nodded. 'But we haven't changed, have we? And the easing of the finances wouldn't be the only consideration in living together, would it?'

She drew in her breath. 'When we get together for our real discussion on this divorce it's going to take more than a couple of hours, Euan!'

He gave her a wry smile. 'Exactly! Which is why I didn't want to be rushed into it in the first place.'

She turned away. 'I shouldn't have forced your hand like this. I should have stayed in London over Christmas and—'

He put his hand on her waist and swung her round to face him. 'I must admit I was annoyed when you first arrived, but now...'

She held her breath as he stood, looking down at her.

'But now, I'm enjoying getting to know you again. I...I've missed you, Carol.'

She breathed out again, a long, yearning sigh. 'And I've missed you, Euan.'

'Have you?'

He seemed surprised.

'Did you get the card I sent you from Bali?' she asked

impulsively, warmed by the rise in emotional temperature.

He looked puzzled. 'No. Maybe it went astray when I was moving apartments in London. What did it say?'

'I can't remember now. It wasn't important. I just happened to think about you when I was sitting under a palm tree on a rather exotic beach.'

He gave her a rakish grin. 'Did it say, "wish you were here"?'

She laughed. 'Nothing as corny as that.' She was trying to keep her voice light, part of her still wanting to protect herself behind the emotional barrier she'd erected.

'I think it's time we went back to work,' she said quickly. 'And you ought to be returning to the dining room.' She hesitated. 'Do you have to stay on duty all night, Euan? I would have thought, as a consultant, you'd be going home soon.'

'I agreed to stay all night,' he said evenly. 'There was a shortage of staff and, besides, living in the medical residents' quarters isn't much like home. I feel more at home in the hospital.'

'That's partly why I came out tonight, if I'm honest,' Carol said. 'Oh, the Golden Fleece is very comfortable but, like you said, it's not home.'

'Not like our shoe-box of a flat!' Euan said, with a wry grin.

Carol took a deep breath. 'I don't think we should go down memory lane any more tonight, Euan.'

She took a step towards the door and this time he held it open for her.

Out in the corridor she heard the buzz of voices and the clanking of trolleys. She smelt that indefinable medical smell that pervaded the hospital, a mixture of a variety of antiseptic lotions.

She'd been dying to go to the loo since halfway through the Christmas dinner so she nipped into the staff cloakroom. Examining herself in the mirror over the wash-basins, she was surprised to see that she still looked perfectly normal. The emotional turmoil going on inside didn't show.

She splashed cold water on her face and dabbed at it with a paper towel, glad that she'd had the sense to use only a light smattering of make-up tonight. Most of it had disappeared. She slipped her lipstick out of her uniform pocket, remembering a former sister tutor who'd told her nursing group that it was the duty of the nurse to look bright and cheerful at all times to help cheer up the patients.

As she outlined her lips she remembered the other old battle-axe sister who thought that nurses shouldn't wear any make-up on duty. Well, she needed this spot of lipstick tonight to boost her own morale, which was in danger of—

The loud siren shriek of the emergency bell interrupted her thoughts and she shot out of the cloakroom door, almost colliding with a couple of nurses who were hurrying in the same direction. The emergency bell in Accident and Emergency was only set off for something very serious.

CHAPTER FOUR

LIGHTS were flashing outside the resuscitation room. Carol hurried inside. Euan was already there, bending over the prone figure of a man. She moved towards the table and leaned across towards Euan.

He raised his head from the patient and said, 'Cardiac arrest! He needs oxygen. Get an ambubag, adrenaline, atropine and lignocaine.'

As Carol hastily assembled the necessary life-saving drugs and equipment, Euan, having placed the heels of both hands on top of one another, was performing cardiac massage on the lower part of the patient's breastbone, depressing it firmly and then releasing it in a continual rhythm.

She saw that Euan had already fixed an airway into the patient's mouth. Quickly, she placed the mouthpiece of the black, balloon-like ambubag in position. Her eyes met Euan's above the patient's prone figure as she synchronised her movements with his.

He was depressing the patient's chest in a steady rhythm of sixty depressions per minute. She squeezed the ambubag once to every four depressions on the chest, sending the life-saving oxygen down into the lungs.

Fay had joined them and was administering the adrenaline, atropine and lignocaine through one of the openings in the venflon, a special hypodermic needle which the paramedics had already attached to the patient's hand.

Carol knew that the adrenaline and atropine would help to speed up the heart's reaction to treatment.

Lignocaine would reduce the excitability of the heart muscle which, at the moment, was feebly quivering like a jelly, with the result that there were no effective heartbeats to pump blood round the patient's circulatory system.

The venflon had two openings. Through the second opening the paramedics had fixed a steady infusion of dextrose to help counteract the shock of the cardiac arrest.

Crucial minutes passed. Carol realised she was holding her breath as she watched for signs of life from her patient. Behind her, near the door, she heard the quiet sobbing of the man's wife.

Staff Nurse Hannah Gregs had placed a chair for the distraught, middle-aged woman to sit on, but she insisted on standing up so she could see what was going on. Suddenly it was all too much for her. She moved forward towards the table.

Carol felt someone touch her arm and heard the inevitable question. 'Is he going to be all right, Nurse?'

'Don't worry—we're doing all we can,' Carol said gently, still keeping her eyes on the patient as she maintained the rhythmic squeezing of the ambubag. 'Would you like to talk to me about your husband?'

She recognised that if the patient's wife had something to occupy her she wouldn't panic so much.

Across the patient's still form she could see Euan, breathing ever more rapidly as he exerted the strong rhythmic pressure on the chest needed to kick-start the heart.

There was still no sign of life.

She caught the worried expression in Euan's eyes and knew that he was wondering if it would be necessary to open up the patient's chest. They could only leave it a few more seconds before...

'My husband's called Bob Moore,' the worried lady at her elbow said, choking back her tears. 'I'm Jean Moore. We've got four children and seven grandchildren and—'

At that precise moment their patient gave a loud, spluttering noise and opened his eyes.

Carol leaned forward, swiftly removing the ambubag and airway from her patient's mouth. He gave another loud splutter, before starting to breathe naturally on his own.

Euan leaned back and rubbed his aching hands together, beads of sweat standing out on his forehead. Carol could hear his rasping breath and knew that he must be feeling exhausted.

Carol was now able to take her eyes momentarily from the patient, and glanced at his wife. She saw a small, plump, middle-aged woman with long, greying hair, swept back behind her ears, who was now grasping her husband's hand and sobbing, 'Bob, can you hear me?'

'Where am I?' Bob Moore said in a shaky voice.

Euan's eyes registered relief as he looked across at Carol and said, 'You're in hospital, Bob.'

'He's had a heart attack, hasn't he, Doctor?' Jean Moore said as she clung to her husband's cold hand.

'Yes, I'm afraid he has,' Euan said gently. 'We'll need to keep him in hospital for a while so that we can find out exactly what triggered it. Don't worry—we'll take good care of him.'

'Can I stay with him, Nurse?' Jean Moore asked Carol.

Carol put an arm round Mrs Moore's shoulder and patted her gently. 'Of course you can. Your husband will want you to be with him.'

The swing doors were opening. Geoff Buxton and

Brian Potter, consultant and junior registrar from the cardiac firm, had arrived.

'Thanks, Euan.' Geoff Buxton, still in theatre greens with his mask under his chin, was striding over to examine their patient. 'I was at a crucial stage in an operation when I heard the emergency bell. I knew you'd cope until I could get here.'

'Have you got a bed in the coronary care unit?' Euan asked.

'Yes, we have,' Brian Potter said.

'I'll get a porter for the transfer,' Carol said.

'And you'd better accompany the patient, Staff Nurse,' Mr Buxton said to Carol. 'Dr Potter will come with you and start treatment in the coronary care unit. I need to go back to Theatre for a while.'

As Carol walked with Dr Brian Potter along the corridor, she kept one hand to steady the progress of the trolley.

'Slow down a bit,' she advised the young porter quietly.

Her patient had successfully survived his first heart attack but he wasn't out of the woods. She glanced at the small, worried-looking woman on the other side of the trolley and gave her a reassuring smile.

Jean Moore's worried expression softened and she smiled back as she said, 'There we were, all the family, having a bit of a party. Bob was as right as rain and the next thing he was on the floor. I thought he'd gone. I grabbed the phone and dialled 999. They were very quick but, all the same, it seemed like a lifetime till we got here. Thank goodness that nice young doctor revived him!'

Nice young doctor! Carol thought. Euan would like that. She might even tell him later on if they got together over a coffee or something. It was going to be a long night in more ways than one.

Brian Potter was holding open the doors of the coronary care unit. Carol handed over her patient to Sister Jane Benthorpe, one of the nurses she remembered from her training days. She'd been in the set above Carol.

'Great to see you back, Carol,' Jane said, as they settled their patient into bed.

'I'm only working here for the night,' Carol said quickly. 'Helping out in the flu epidemic.'

'Pity! We could do with some of the old-timers back at the Moortown General.'

Mercifully, Jane didn't go through the routine questioning about Carol's relationship with Euan. Brian Potter had started to examine their patient and Carol left, after reassuring Bob's wife that they would do everything they could to make her husband well again.

She made her way along the deserted corridor. Through the windows she could see a full moon, shining down over the rooftops of Moortown. Some people would still be out on the town; others would be dreaming about what Christmas Day held for them. All those family get-togethers which had to be enjoyed—or endured, in some cases!

She remembered her mother telling her, just before she died, that when she'd given birth to Carol on Christmas morning she'd been glad she had an excuse not to have to cook the Christmas dinner. But she'd also reassured her that she'd been thrilled to have a baby at long last, after enduring eight miscarriages.

Eight miscarriages! It was frightening to even think about it. How her mother must have suffered!

She was passing the children's ward and her mind turned to little Adam, her patient with the high temperature and possible meningitis. Quickly, she pushed open the swing doors and went inside to see if she could get an update on his condition.

Sister Ann Threadgold was near the door, giving a drink to a little tousle-haired girl. She settled her patient and came over to see Carol, who waited by the desk.

When Carol asked how Adam was, Ann took her into the side ward. He was sleeping, his rapid breathing noisy. Carol leaned over the bed and put her hand on the little boy's forehead. It was still very hot. She glanced at the temperature chart. One hundred and one.

'It's coming down,' she whispered to Anne.

Anne nodded. 'Yes, the penicillin seems to be working.'

'Have we got the report of his tests back from the lab?'

'Not yet. Would you like me to let you know the results when I get them?'

'Yes, please.'

Carol smoothed a lock of Adam's damp, fair hair away from his eyes and turned to leave.

'How's it going down there?' Ann asked in a casual tone.

'It's always busy on Christmas Eve,' Carol said quickly, one hand on the door.

Ann smiled. 'No, I didn't mean the patients. You're working with Euan again, aren't you? Are you—?'

'Sorry, Ann. Must dash. Talk to you later.'

Hurrying back to A and E, she realised that she must have given the grapevine something to work on, by turning up tonight! The whole hospital must be alive with speculation about her and Euan.

Pushing open the swing doors that led into A and E, she saw that the majority of the activity in the department was centred around the entrance. An ambulance screeched to a halt. The waiting porters moved forward with their trolleys.

At that moment, Euan came out of the treatment room. He seemed relieved to see her.

'There's been a two-car collision,' he told her tersely. 'The paramedics are bringing the casualties in now. I don't know how many but the orthopaedic firm should arrive to help us any minute. They've finished dealing with the earlier car-crash patients.'

Carol followed him towards the main entrance. Fay was organising her nursing staff, instructing which nurse was to deal with which patient. The ambulance doors opened and a couple of paramedics began to unload a stretcher.

A second ambulance swung into the parking bay. Porters rushed forward, and Euan instructed his medical staff which area of A and E they were to work in.

The orthopaedic team arrived—tall, grey-haired consultant, Frank Webster, senior registrar, Derek Green, and their two young house surgeons, Victoria Christie and Ray Pelman.

Carol was assigned to help Frank Webster fix a badly mutilated leg onto a splint. The patient had lost a lot of blood.

'Shall I get a blood sample so that we'll know which type of blood to give him, Mr Webster?' she said, as she cut through the tattered clothing to expose the limb.

'Yes. I'll need to get him into Theatre as quickly as possible,' Frank Webster told her as she reached for the phone to call the lab.

As Carol put the phone down, after giving her instructions, she noticed the worried expression on the consultant's face. Examining the leg more closely, she could see that the injury was extensive. She doubted very much if they would be able to save the leg, but Frank

Webster was an expert orthopaedic surgeon so there was still hope.

She filled a bowl with a soapy solution of Cetavalon and water and began to clean the blood from the patient's face, revealing a small cut above his eye. Quickly, she pulled the edges of the cut together and inserted a couple of stitches.

Their patient only looked about twenty and she was glad that he was still mercifully unconscious. His respiration was strong and rhythmical. He might recover consciousness soon.

'Do we know anything about this young man, Mr Webster?' she asked.

The orthopaedic consultant was frowning as he continued his examination of the badly mutilated leg. 'The paramedics said he was the driver of one of the cars,' he said. He peeled off his surgical gloves and raised his head to look at Carol.

'The engine came through onto his leg on impact. A young woman, sitting on the back seat, has survived with a broken upper arm—fractured humerus is the provisional diagnosis. She's able to give some details. She's on that trolley over there. Would you find out what you can about our patient while I fix up a glucose saline drip?'

The young woman, though in a state of shock, was able to tell Carol that the patient with the badly injured leg was her boyfriend and he was called Ryan Brown.

'He will be all right, won't he, Nurse? I mean, he's not going to lose that leg, is he? He's a brilliant footballer. He plays for Moortown. You must have heard of him.'

Carol swallowed the lump in her throat. 'We're doing all we can,' she said, which was the only truthful statement she could make at the moment. 'Mr Webster is going to take Ryan into Theatre and operate on him. May I have your name, please?'

'Samantha Crabtree,' she replied.

Carol was suddenly aware that Euan was standing beside her. 'We need to X-ray your arm, Samantha,' he said to the patient. 'Will you arrange that, Carol, and then come and help me in cubicle two?'

'It really hurts, Doctor,' Samantha said, twisting her face in an agonised grimace. 'Can you give me something for the pain?'

'You've already had one painkilling injection, Samantha,' Euan said gently, studying the paramedics' scribbled notes, 'but I'll give you something stronger that will help you.'

Carol swabbed Samantha's skin and handed Euan a kidney dish with the required syringe. Having given the painkilling injection, he went off in the direction of cubicle two. Carol asked one of the extra nurses who'd been drafted in from the wards to take Samantha for an X-ray of her upper arm.

After making sure that Samantha knew exactly what was going to happen, she went back to report her findings to Frank Webster.

'Thanks, Staff Nurse. I'm going to take Ryan up to Theatre now. There's a chance I may have to amputate but I'll do what I can to patch things up if it's at all possible.'

Carol drew in her breath. 'I hope he won't need an amputation, sir. Apparently, Ryan plays football for Moortown.'

She saw a flash of anxiety cross Frank Webster's mature face. 'Of course,' he said softly. 'I knew the name Ryan Brown rang a bell when you told me just now.' He put both hands over his cheeks, remaining motionless for a few seconds. 'Well, I can only do my best,' he said briskly. 'I can't perform miracles.'

'I've heard you can,' Carol said quietly, hoping she wasn't overstepping the mark.

The surgeon raised one eyebrow as he looked at her. 'You could be right. On the assessment of my first examination, it will be nothing short of a miracle if I can save that leg.'

As Carol went into cubicle two to help Euan, she tried to put Ryan Brown's impending operation from her mind.

A young boy of about twelve was lying on the examination couch.

'Concussion,' Euan said, as Carol joined him. 'I've given him a thorough examination—his bone structure seems intact and there's no apparent internal injury. He's called Charlie and he's the younger brother of Ryan, the driver, apparently.'

Their patient's eyes were opening. He squinted up at the bright lights, before closing his eyes again.

'Charlie, can you hear me?' Euan said.

The boy muttered something incoherent.

'You're in hospital, Charlie,' Carol said, reaching down to take hold of her patient's wrist so that she could check his pulse rate.

'Pulse rate only sixty,' she said to Euan, 'but it's strong.'

He nodded. 'I noticed his pulse was slow when I examined him, which would, hopefully, suggest that he hasn't got any internal bleeding. We'll have him admitted to Male Medical for observation. Would you like to take him up there, Carol? Give them the details of the case and ask if they'll let me know when he's fully conscious.'

That was typical of Euan, Carol thought as she went

in search of a porter and a trolley. He always liked to keep tabs on the patients who passed through his hands. Even though Charlie was now technically under the care of the medical team, Euan would still have him at the back of his mind.

Her patient stirred fitfully as they went up in the lift to Male Medical. She tried squeezing his hand but there was no response. As she smoothed her fingers over his forehead she was rewarded by the opening of his eyes.

'Who are you?' he said.

'I'm Carol. Who are you?'

'I'm Charlie,' came the faint but reassuring reply. At least he hadn't forgotten who he was. 'Can I have a drink?'

Relief flooded through her as the boy spoke. 'Yes, of course you can, Charlie. As soon as we get to the ward.'

Charlie closed his eyes again. 'Do they have any Coca-Cola?' he muttered.

Carol smiled. 'I don't know, but I'm sure they'll be able to find you some orange squash.'

'That's kid's stuff!' the twelve-year-old told her. 'Where's Ryan?'

'He's going to spend the night in hospital as well,' she said quickly.

'Can I see him?' Charlie said in a small voice.

'Not just at the moment. He's asleep.'

This seemed to satisfy her patient, who remained quiet until they reached the medical ward.

Carol explained the details of the case to Sister Jill Backhouse, one of the newer sisters who'd arrived at Moortown after Carol left. Helen Caldwell, the medical senior registrar, arrived and began to examine Charlie, who was now chatting and asking lots of questions.

'On the way up Charlie asked for a drink of Coca-Cola,' Carol told Sister Backhouse.

'He'll have to make do with orange squash,' Jill Backhouse said abruptly.

Carol gave a wry smile. 'That's what I told him. Well, good luck! I have a feeling Charlie won't be fobbed off lightly.'

She said goodbye to her young patient and set off back to A and E, where she found that the situation had eased considerably—so much so that Euan's two young housemen, Rod Grant and Geoff Bailey, had been sent away to try and get some sleep.

Ryan Brown had been taken up to Theatre to have his leg operated on by Frank Webster. Ryan's girlfriend, Samantha, was also up in Theatre, waiting to have an operation on her upper arm to fix a fractured bone.

The remaining four car-crash patients had been admitted to the orthopaedic wards, where their various non-urgent injuries would be reviewed in the morning.

'Your friend phoned,' Euan said quietly. He was standing just inside his office.

His enigmatic eyes were giving nothing away as he gave her more details. 'Dr Richard Courtland, the man who phoned earlier. Fay asked me to take the call. He's going to call back.'

'But it's nearly two o'clock in the morning!' Carol said, her face colouring.

'I expect the poor man can't sleep for thinking about you,' Euan said lightly.

'Euan, I've told you I'm not having a relationship with Richard,' she said forcefully.

He took hold of her arm. 'Better come inside before the whole department hears you.'

He closed the door behind them and stood, looking down at her, his hand still on her arm. She felt his hot breath, fanning her face. Looking up at him now, she thought she'd never seen him look so handsome.

'I know it sounds corny, but Richard and I are just good friends,' she said quietly.

'Maybe that's the way you feel, but I think lover boy sees it differently.'

'Euan, I—'

The phone started to ring. As Euan went over to his desk Carol knew exactly how important it was to convince Euan that Richard meant nothing to her. Euan was covering the mouthpiece with his hand. 'Carol, it's Dr Richard Courtland again.'

A wave of apprehension swept over her. Euan was holding out the receiver. As if in a dream, she walked across to the desk. Euan prepared to leave.

She put out her hand. 'Don't go, Euan!'

'I have to!' he said brusquely. He turned at the door, running a hand through his dark hair. 'It's better if you speak to him alone.'

She watched the door closing as she began to speak. 'Richard, it's nearly two o'clock in the morning and—'

'Carol, I wanted to talk to you. You said you were going to contact your solicitor friend about your divorce while you were up in Moortown. Have you…?'

She gathered from his slurred speech that he'd been drinking. In the background she could hear the noise of chattering voices, laughter and music. He was probably at some all-night party in a London club.

'It's Christmas Eve, Richard, or rather Christmas morning now. We've been very busy here and—'

'Carol, I've called to ask you to marry me.'

She drew in her breath. For the last few weeks she'd had the feeling that Richard's attitude towards her was changing from just-good-friends to something more serious.

'Richard, I've enjoyed our friendship but that's all it was…and that's the way I'd like it to stay.'

'Do you know what I think? I think you're still carrying a torch for that husband of yours. I don't think you've any intention of getting a divorce.'

'We haven't had time for a proper discussion,' she said, 'but whether we divorce or not has got nothing to do with you, Richard.'

'So the answer's definitely no, is it?'

'Afraid so.'

She heard him sniff plaintively, and couldn't decide whether he was putting on an act or was really cut up about her reply. Probably the former, knowing Richard's fickle emotions.

'I'll go and drown my sorrows,' she heard him say.

The music in the background was getting louder. 'You'll survive, Richard.'

As she put the phone down she could imagine how he would go back to the bar and order a large whisky. If the barmaid was pretty he'd probably try to arrange a date.

The door opened and Euan came in. Walking over to his desk, he said, 'I need some help from you, Carol.'

'Yes, I'm sorry I had to take that phone call,' she said quickly, as she began to walk over to the door.

He put out his hand and touched her arm. 'Was the call important?'

She shook her head. 'No. I think Richard had been celebrating and drank one too many.'

'Well, it is Christmas Eve.' He was looking down at her, his deeply expressive eyes searching her face.

'It's Christmas morning,' she said quietly. 'Ten minutes to two, to be exact.'

'And that's why I need your help. I promised to go over to the nurses' home for the last few minutes of the Christmas dance if I wasn't needed here. Everything's quiet at the moment.'

She moved away. His fingers on her arm had seemed like fire.

'We can hold the fort until you get back, Euan so—'

'Fay's got everything under control. I'd like you to come with me to the dance. There's only ten minutes left so...'

'But why me? Everybody will start asking questions.'

Her heart was literally thumping, and her throat had gone dry. Looking up at Euan now, she couldn't think why he would want them to be seen together...unless...

'I was going to take Fay but she wants to get on with her report while it's quiet. She suggested I might twist your arm into going.'

Her spirits, which had been rising, now dropped again. She was second choice!

'It's traditional for the consultants to turn up at the nurses' dance if they're still here, and they're always accompanied by a female member of the medical staff. Come on, Carol. Ten minutes...now nine!'

Her emotions were in turmoil as she allowed herself to be propelled towards the door and into Fay's office.

Fay looked up from the report she was writing. 'Oh, good! You've persuaded Carol. Well, get a move on, Euan, because they'll be finishing in a few minutes and your name will be mud if you let the nurses down. Take my cloak, Carol. It's freezing out there!'

Carol wrapped the black, red-lined, woollen cloak around her as they hurried out of the main entrance and began to cross the hospital forecourt to the nurses' home. The ambulances were lined up like sentinels, waiting for the next call to duty. As she breathed out she could see her own breath, looking like a cloud of smoke.

Euan put his arm lightly on her shoulders and then drew her against him as they hurried along. It felt so natural to snuggle under his shoulder as she always had done in those far-off days. A cynical voice in her head told her that Euan was only wearing a suit so that was why he was holding her against him. Whatever the reason, she knew she was enjoying the few seconds of physical contact with him.

He drew away as they reached the wide stone steps of the nurses' home. Going through the revolving glass and wooden doors, she felt a rush of nostalgia.

The main entrance hadn't changed since she'd enrolled as a young eighteen-year-old. She looked up at the high ceiling, stretching up to the first-floor bedrooms. The tiled floor of the lobby gave way to the steps leading to the main hall where, through the open doors, she could see people dancing.

She paused for a moment and Euan waited for her as she stood stock still.

'So many memories!' she breathed.

Euan looked down at her and smiled. 'Come on, we can't live on memories,' he said huskily.

Gently he put his fingers under her chin and tilted her face so that she had to look into his eyes. There was an expression of real tenderness in his eyes. For a moment she thought he was going to kiss her. He bent forward.

'Let me take your cloak,' he said.

Stifling her disappointment, she shrugged off the heavy cloak and watched as he hung it on one of the nearby hooks.

'Ready?' he asked with a bright, socially orientated smile.

Carol smiled back. It would be best to look confident and in control when she made her entrance with Euan. She planned to fob off any unwanted questions about her relationship with him because, if she were honest with herself, her emotions were now so confused that she was incapable of answering the questions even to herself.

'Mr Maitland! So glad you could make it.'

A red-headed sister, still in uniform, claimed Euan the moment he stepped inside, and pulled him onto the dance floor.

Looking around, Carol could see that about half the nursing staff were still in uniform, the others in various festive-season outfits. She was beginning to feel tired after her long day. Euan obviously didn't need her now so she decided to keep a low profile and get her breath back.

Moving into an unoccupied corner, she smoothed the skirt of her royal blue uniform dress, pulled a tissue from her pocket and bent to dab at a bloodstain on her shoe.

'Well, how did Cinderella manage to escape to the Ball? Last time we met you were hard at it in A and E.'

Drat! She'd been noticed. She straightened to see Phil Morton, Euan's senior registrar, smiling down at her.

'Euan asked me to come with him but once here I became the proverbial wallflower.'

'What a waste!' Phil said, as he held out his hand and pulled her towards the dance floor. 'Ah, the traditional last waltz. Did you learn how to do this?'

His ebullient high spirits were infectious. She decided she mustn't be churlish. She forced a smile as Phil whirled her into the middle of the room.

'My mother insisted I had dancing lessons when I was small,' she told Phil breathlessly. 'And this waltz thing was one of them. I remember having to count one-two-three, one-two-three...'

'Oops, sorry!' Phil said, as he planted a large foot on top of Carol's. 'Are you OK?'

She winced and laughed at the same time as she warmed to the endearing Phil.

'Good thing you're not as clumsy as that with your

patients,' she told him as they continued haltingly around the floor.

'If I were, your dear husband would soon have me booted out. He can be very exacting where medical standards are concerned.'

'How did you know he was my husband?' she asked, carefully avoiding Phil's feet in the crush.

He smiled. 'It's all round the hospital. They're placing bets on whether you'll get back together again. It's my bet you will!'

'Look, Phil,' she began carefully, 'it's all very complicated so—'

'I know. Euan and I went out for a few beers together soon after I got my job here. It's a well-known fact that alcohol loosens the tongue but it's usually the truth. You know what they say, *in vino veritas*. Well, Euan poured out his heart to me after he'd had a few and I thought—' Phil stopped in mid-sentence as someone from behind tapped him on the shoulder.

Carol, engrossed in what Phil was saying, had only seen Euan at the last moment.

'What did you think, Phil?' Euan asked evenly.

'I thought...' Phil looked first at Euan, then at Carol, took a deep breath and said, 'I think it's your dance, sir.'

Euan gave him a wry grin. 'You're dead right about that. I was planning to cut in so I'm glad you made it easy for me.'

As Euan drew her towards him, Carol was left wondering what he'd said on the occasion when he'd poured out his heart to Phil.

'I was beginning to think there wouldn't be time for a dance with you.'

Euan's words cut through her conjecture and she looked up at him. The feel of his arms, holding her, was infinitely disturbing. Every bone in her body seemed fluid as she leaned against him, her feet moving automatically in time with the music.

She'd always enjoyed dancing with him. His movements were so relaxed; it was so easy to follow him. She remembered the dancing lessons she'd had all those years ago. When she'd asked the teacher how she would know which way to move, she'd been told that the position of the man's hips would guide her.

She could feel Euan's hips against hers now, and sensual sensations were sweeping over her. She was oblivious to everything around her as she allowed herself to be propelled across the dance floor.

He bent his head and whispered in her ear. 'This may be the last time we dance together.'

'Yes, it might…unless…'

'Unless what, Carol?' he prompted, his voice husky.

'Mr Maitland, will you draw the ticket for the main raffle prize?'

It was the red-headed sister again.

'Sorry to interrupt,' she said to Carol, 'but we need Mr Maitland up on stage. He promised.'

The music had stopped. Carol blinked as the lights came up again. Euan released her from his arms, but he was still watching her intently.

'Wait for me,' he said quietly. 'This won't take long.'

CHAPTER FIVE

IN THE main lobby of the nurses' home Euan reached for Carol's cloak and placed it around her shoulders. Nurses were streaming past them, chattering and laughing as they returned to their rooms. The nurses who lived out were going to the waiting cars and taxis. One or two glances were sent in their direction but Carol made a deliberate effort not to make eye contact with anyone.

They went out through the revolving door, down the steps and started to walk towards the main entrance of the hospital.

Suddenly, Euan stopped walking and turned to look at Carol in the bright moonlight. A car zoomed past her and she was temporarily dazzled by the headlights.

He put out both hands and placed them on either side of her arms, his fingers gripping her through the thick woollen material of her cloak.

'Remember how we used to walk in the nurses' home garden? Let's go and see if the roses are still in bloom.'

She laughed. 'In December? Have we time?'

'Fay will phone me from A and E if there's an emergency and Phil Morton's already gone back there.'

As they walked along the narrow, crunchy, gravel path she could almost imagine the scent of the roses that bloomed on either side during the summer. Small lights at ground level illuminated the rose bushes, which now looked sad and neglected in their pruned, barren, winter state.

Euan took out a large white handkerchief and wiped it over a seat. The wooden slats of the seat felt cold even through her cape as she sat down. Euan took hold of her hands, rubbing them in his own.

'We mustn't stay long, Carol. Your hands are frozen!'

The light of the full moon and the illumination from the small path lights was enough to outline the earnest expression on his face. She hadn't seen him look so caringly at her since the early days of their marriage. She remembered, in that far-off former life, how he would make her sit down when she had a problem and they would talk it through. But that had been long before their discussions had changed to bitter arguments.

The touch of his fingers, warming hers, was totally unnerving. She took a deep breath as she tried to come to terms with her conflicting emotions. He pulled her against him, and in spite of the cold she could feel herself melting inside. She wanted this moment to go on for ever. No arguments, no everyday problems of living. Just the two of them, cocooned in unreality.

But life isn't like that, is it? said the still small voice of reason inside her head. Euan's financial circumstances had changed but he was still Euan and she was still Carol and, as Euan had said, they would have to agree to differ.

He bent his head and kissed her gently on the lips. She closed her eyes to savour the moment.

She breathed out a long, luxurious sigh of happiness.

'It's just like the old days, sitting here with you, Euan. If only—'

She broke off, unable to finish what was uppermost in her mind.

'If only life was always like this,' he prompted, his fingers gripping her shoulders and his expressive eyes searching her face. 'Where did we go wrong? How did we get from that idyllic state to a situation where half the time it was open warfare?'

'And, what is more to the point,' she said quietly, 'if

we were to try again, would the whole structure of our marriage collapse again?'

His fingers gripped more tightly. 'That's what we have to decide. We can't simply say the marriage broke down. A marriage can't break down unless one or both of the partners makes it happen.'

She turned her face towards him. 'I never wanted it to break down, Euan. I didn't plan to walk out like that.'

'Didn't you?'

In the moonlight, she could see the arching of one of his eyebrows. She put out her hand and touched his face, smoothing her fingers over the beginnings of a dark stubble on his chin.

'I simply couldn't bear any more bickering over silly little things,' she said heatedly. 'Oh, the big problems were always there in the background but it was the everyday, unimportant things like…like…'

He was smiling at her now. 'Like your refusal to squeeze the toothpaste from the bottom instead of the middle?'

She smiled back. 'But did it matter?'

'It did to me…at the time. But I can see now that I shouldn't have gone on about it.'

He pulled her closer to him. 'One thing I know for sure, as I said when we were talking to Janet, I can't change my personality any more than you can. We can both modify to a certain extent, we can agree to differ, but we have to be sure—'

He broke off as his mobile shrilled insistently.

'Damn!' He took the phone from his pocket.

'Yes, Fay… I'll be right there… Yes, she's here, too…'

He rose, and as he helped her to her feet he drew her against him.

'Fay needs us. We've got to go back,' he said evenly, as he pulled himself away.

Waves of emotional frustration swept over her as they hurried back along the path and out into the brightly lit area in front of A and E. Just when they had really started to talk about what mattered!

With an effort she reminded herself that she was on duty.

Euan dropped her hand as they went in through the main doors. She took a deep breath as she put herself back into a working mood.

Fay was suturing a superficial stab wound on a young man in cubicle one. Next door Phil was setting up an intravenous drip on the other young man involved in the street brawl who had internal abdominal wounds.

'There's another motorbike casualty coming in,' Fay said, looking up from her suturing. 'That sounds like the ambulance now.'

Carol followed Euan to the main doors. The back doors of the ambulance opened, and a paramedic wheeled the patient in.

'His name's Dave Connor,' the paramedic told them. 'Age seventeen, going home from a disco, went round a bend too quickly. Looks like his thigh bone's taken a knock. I've given him some pethidine.'

'I'll phone Orthopaedics,' Carol said, as Euan took over from the paramedic.

Seconds later she was back with Euan. 'Orthopaedics are still tied up with the patients from that two-car crash. They'll send one of the team when they can be spared. Frank Webster is still in Theatre, working on our young footballer's leg. I hope they don't have to amputate it.'

Euan raised his eyebrows. 'It looked pretty bad, but Frank can sometimes work miracles.'

'That's what I told him,' she said.

Euan was stroking his chin thoughtfully as he looked down at their new patient. 'Tell me where it hurts, Dave,' he said in a sympathetic tone.

The young man pointed to his thigh. 'That's where I hit the ground and... Ouch... I can't move it.'

'Keep still while I have a look,' Euan said.

Carol was already cutting through Dave's tangled, bloodstained jeans. The skin around the painful area of the thigh was purple and dark red but the bone wasn't protruding.

'Get an X-ray, Carol,' Euan said. 'I'll check on those two stab victims while you're away.'

Returning with her patient, Carol handed over the X-rays to Euan. He frowned as he put them up on the lighted screen.

'A break in the middle of his thighbone,' he said. 'Dave will need to go to Theatre as soon as Frank Webster can take him. Call Theatre, Carol.'

She made her phone call and returned to report to Euan. 'Frank Webster's team is still busy. He's suggesting we use Theatre Two and get on with the operation ourselves.'

Euan pulled a wry face. 'I should never have told Frank I specialised in orthopaedics before I went into general surgery. OK, let's go!'

Theatre Sister hovered at the edge of Theatre Two as Carol took her place beside Euan. Ray Pelman, one of the orthopaedic house surgeons, had been drafted in from Theatre One, but Euan, being the more senior surgeon, was in charge. A couple of theatre nurses were working between the two rooms. An anaesthetist on call had been roused from his bed and now stood at the head of the table, checking his equipment.

Carol heard the swing doors close as Sister went back

to her other patient. She was on her own. She'd assisted in minor operations in the ship's well-equipped hospital but it was more than two years since she'd been in Theatre here at Moortown. But she found it was all coming back to her. Her extensive training here was standing her in good stead.

Their patient was undergoing the operation on a special orthopaedic bed which could be transferred intact to the ward. After the preliminary incisions Carol handed Euan the sterile Steinmann's pin, a specially constructed piece of orthopaedic equipment which would hold the injured leg in the correct position. Carefully, he inserted it into the patient's leg, underneath the knee.

'OK, now we'll set up the traction equipment that will hold the broken ends of the thigh bone together,' Euan said.

Carol helped to fix the injured leg into the traction equipment while Euan adjusted the correct amount of pull required to keep the leg in the best position. He stood back from the orthopaedic bed for a moment as if to satisfy himself that he'd got it right. Seconds later he was nodding.

'Yes, that should align the two ends of bone and start the healing process,' he said. Pulling down his mask, he looked at Carol.

'Thanks for your help. Now, would you like to take Dave to the orthopaedic ward?'

Their eyes met. They had been ultra-professional with each other during the operation, but as Carol looked at Euan she could see a warmth in his eyes that hadn't been there when she'd first arrived this evening. Her spirits lifted. They were making progress.

In the fragmented time they'd spent together had they really managed to begin the healing process of their marriage? She didn't dare to think about it in her busy state. She had to get through the night.

As soon as she'd settled Dave in the orthopaedic ward, Carol returned to A and E to find that the workload was easing off. Fay and Euan were in the office, making a report on the patients who'd been admitted during the night.

'Have we had an update from Obstetrics on the baby who was born in cubicle three, Carol?' Euan asked, as she walked through the door.

Carol perched herself on the side of Fay's desk as she mentally went rapidly through the number of internal phone messages she'd taken.

She knew Euan always insisted on a follow-up, although, strictly speaking, it was the consultant in charge of the department the patients were sent to who should have taken over responsibility. It was typical of the way he took his medical work very seriously.

'We've checked out all the other patients,' Fay said. 'I wondered if there was a message you hadn't reported.'

Carol shook her head. 'No, I always write everything down, even if it's only a scribbled note to myself to be recorded later. And I wouldn't have forgotten a report about that dear little baby girl. I remember, Euan and I were next door to you, Fay, in cubicle two, treating that motorbike patient, Brad Somers, the one with the fractured tib and fib that we set in a long leg plaster.'

'It sounded like a quick delivery, Fay,' Euan said.

Fay gave a wry smile. 'It was! The head had barely crowned before the rest of the body shot out into my hands.'

Carol smiled as a mental image of the little baby girl flashed through her mind.

The mother was young with long blonde hair, she re-

membered, and the look of serene happiness on her face
had been very moving. She'd found herself turning away
to stop the familiar yearnings taking over.

'Give me a copy of the notes about the baby's birth.
I'll call Obstetrics, if you like, and get a report,' she said
quickly.

'Thanks,' Fay said. 'Would you like a coffee?'

Carol smiled. 'Anything to keep me awake will be
most welcome.'

Picking up the phone, she punched in the digits for
Obstetrics.

'Sister Knowles speaking,' came the immediate reply.

She had a mental image of the tall, brown-haired,
Australian sister who'd joined the Moortown staff about
four years ago. A thoroughly competent professional,
she also had a great sense of humour and Carol had
enjoyed being in her company on many occasions.

'Barbara, it's Carol Maitland in A and E,' she began.
'We're checking—'

'Carol! I hoped I'd get a chance to speak to you. What
a surprise to see you at the midnight dinner! I was just
about to come over for a chat when you disappeared.
Are you and Euan—?'

'Barbara, we're a bit busy right now,' Carol cut in
quickly, as she glanced at the baby's case notes. 'So if
you could just give me a brief update on Laurie Gibson's
baby. The little girl who was born here in A and E...'

She paused as her eyes caught sight of Euan's scrawl
at the bottom of the case notes. Apparently, the mother
had told him she was going to call the baby Holly because she was born on Christmas Eve and there was a
branch of holly over the door of cubicle three in A and
E. Ah! What a lovely idea!

'The baby's name's Holly,' she continued, watching
Fay spooning instant coffee into three mugs.

Her eyelids felt droopy. She really needed that coffee to boost her energy level! Night duty was a strain when you hadn't slept during the preceding day.

Euan was drumming his fingers on the desk, his pen poised to take down the information.

Seconds passed and there was no reply from the other end.

'Barbara, are you still there?' Carol asked, thinking that perhaps the connection might have been broken.

'Baby Holly isn't here. I thought she was down in A and E with you,' came the chilling reply.

Carol felt as if the hairs on the back of her neck were standing up. There must be some mistake. She swallowed hard. 'What made you think baby Holly might be with us?' she asked, her voice wavering.

Out of the corner of her eye she saw Fay put down the coffee tin and spoon. Euan had leapt to his feet and was holding out his hand for the receiver.

She had barely time to say, 'Euan wants to speak—' before the receiver was taken from her hand.

'What's the problem, Barbara?' Euan said, in a firm, no-nonsense voice.

Carol leaned closer, trying to catch what Barbara was saying.

Euan was frowning. 'Of course I didn't send for baby Holly... Yes, I know I insist on following up my patients but, well, where's the nurse who's supposed to have brought the baby down here?'

He was listening again, his face becoming more and more grim as he listened to what the obstetrics sister was saying.

'I'll call you back,' he said, putting down the phone.

The three of them faced each other round the desk, their anxious faces showing how disturbed they were.

'What's happened?' Fay asked, her voice barely audible.

Euan put the tips of his fingers together as he glanced from one to the other.

'It appears that Barbara Knowles had asked a staff nurse to take special care of baby Holly through the night in the nursery. She was showing a slight touch of yellowing of the skin and Barbara asked the nurse to report if the condition worsened so that they could start phototherapy treatment under the blue lamp.'

He paused as he leaned back in his chair and put his hands behind his dark head. Carol found she was holding her breath. She tried to relax as she waited for him to continue.

'When Barbara got back from the midnight Christmas dinner the staff nurse said she'd taken a call from me, asking if baby Holly could be taken down to A and E for some special tests I was doing on babies born under emergency conditions.'

'No!' Carol put her hands to her face as she listened to the details of the devastating fabrication.

'The staff nurse offered to take baby Holly to A and E on her way to the second sitting of the midnight supper and pick her up on the way back when I would have, supposedly, finished these fictitious tests. She hasn't returned.'

'So, presumably, Barbara thought the nurse was waiting down here with baby Holly for you to finish the tests,' Carol said. 'My God! Holly's been abducted! But who's the nurse involved?'

Euan ran a hand through his dark hair, his eyes anxiously scanning her face.

'Apparently, it was the staff nurse who came down to collect Holly immediately after she was born. I remember she waited in the cubicle until I'd finished my examination.'

'She was tall and blonde, wasn't she?' Carol said.

Euan nodded. 'Yes, do you know her?'

Carol frowned as she racked her brain. 'I might do. There was something familiar about her.'

'Barbara says she's one of the temporary nurses who was drafted in, like yourself, because of the flu epidemic,' Euan said. 'Of course, she'd been thoroughly screened. She had good qualifications and impeccable references and, apparently, she comes from Moortown so they had no reason to question whether—'

'I'll phone Barbara back,' Carol said quickly. 'Maybe I'll know who this nurse is. There must be some mistake. A Moortown nurse wouldn't abduct a baby.'

'I'll talk to the police on the outside line,' Euan said grimly. 'Whoever she is, she's had time to get well clear of the hospital so we'll have to instigate a search. What an awful thing to happen, especially on Christmas Eve!'

As he spoke, Barbara Knowles hurried in through the door.

'I've left my staff nurse in charge,' she said breathlessly.

Carol put down the phone. 'I was just calling you. Does the mother know the baby's missing?'

'No. She's sleeping peacefully. I've got a nurse sitting by her bedside with instructions to contact me as soon as she wakes up. Hopefully, by then we—'

'Who's this mystery staff nurse—the one who took the baby?' Carol cut in. 'If she comes from Moortown I might know her.'

Across the desk she could see Euan, holding a phone in one hand, the other clamped over his ear as he outlined the dilemma to the police.

'Apparently, she was born in Moortown,' Barbara said

in a shaky voice. 'I've brought her certificates and references to show you. Her papers say she trained in London. After qualifying, she went on to specialise in obstetrics.'

Barbara sank onto a chair and placed the papers on the desk. 'Look, it's all there.'

Carol glanced down at the papers. 'Penny Slater, age thirty…' she read.

A vague memory was ticking away in her brain.

'There was a Penny Slater… She was two forms below me in school. I think she did go to London, but that was because the whole family moved down there when she was about fifteen. They lived in Cragdale, quite near me… Now I remember!'

'Remember what?' Euan said. 'The police are on their way so they'll need all the information we can give them.'

Carol swallowed hard. 'Don't you remember Penny Slater, Fay? A tall girl with long dark hair—well, it was in those days.'

Fay shook her head. 'I have difficulty remembering old school chums unless they were in our form, but if she lived near you, Carol, you've got a better chance of remembering her.'

'This nurse has short blonde hair,' Barbara Knowles put in quickly.

Carol ran a hand through her own recently colour rinsed hair.

'She must be blonde from the bottle,' she said, as a mental image of the tall blonde staff nurse, passing her in the doorway of the cubicle, flashed through her mind.

Yes, the tall angular frame was the characteristic which had first alerted her to the fact that she knew this person from way, way back. Penny Slater had always been above average height and very thin. And the high cheekbones and determined mouth had seemed familiar.

She frowned as from the mists of time her memory delivered another piece of relevant information. 'I've just remembered reading a snippet in the local paper about six years ago,' she said slowly. 'Cousin Brenda brought it to my attention—she said she'd never liked the Slater family.'

'Yes, what was it about?' Euan asked.

Carol drew in her breath. 'Apparently, Penny's brother was jailed for forgery.'

She rubbed her hands over her flushed cheeks as she looked across at Euan.

'Are you thinking what I'm thinking?' he said slowly.

She nodded. 'It all ties in, doesn't it?'

Euan picked up the papers. 'They look authentic to me but, then, I'm no expert on forged documents. We'll leave that to the police, talking of which...'

A siren could be heard outside the main entrance.

'The most important thing is that we don't let this disrupt the smooth running of the hospital,' Euan said in his firm, no-nonsense, consultant voice. 'Our priority is to get baby Holly back but we also have to think of all our other patients. Barbara, I'd like you to go back to your ward now. I'll deal with the police.'

It was around three-thirty before the police finished their investigations. They'd interviewed all the medical staff who'd been in contact with Penny Slater. Carol had explained she'd seen Penny collect the baby from cubicle three. She hadn't realised that it was someone she knew from her past, although she had seemed vaguely familiar.

They were, of course, extremely interested in her information about the brother's forgery conviction.

After most of the police had gone, leaving a couple

of officers on duty by the main entrance, Fay asked
Carol if she was feeling OK.

Carol shrugged. 'To be honest, I'm having difficulty,
keeping awake, but—'

'You didn't have a sleep during the day, like I did, so
I'm going to send you off for half an hour. Close your
eyes and have forty winks. You'll be no use to us if you
pass out. All the cubicles are empty so wrap yourself in
a blanket and doze off. I'll wake you up when it's time
to go to tea.'

'I'd forgotten we get a teabreak. Maybe I'll just keep
going until—'

'No, you won't!' Fay said. 'I'm really grateful to you
for coming in to help us out but I don't want you carried
out on a stretcher.'

'I'm so wound up about baby Holly. I can't get her
little face out of my mind. I keep thinking about how
I'd feel if she were mine. I think I'm too anxious to
sleep.'

Fay pointed towards the door. 'Go and lie down,
Carol. Even if you don't sleep your body will be resting.'

Carol forced a smile. 'You're a good friend, Fay.'

She went out of the door and moved slowly along to
cubicle one. She had to pass cubicle three. She glanced
in. It was empty. She had a flash image of baby Holly
in her young mother's arms.

Poor girl! She wondered if she'd been told yet.
Deliberately blanking out the image, she walked into
cubicle one.

The sheet had been changed on the examination
couch. She kicked off her shoes and stretched out under
the aertex blanket. She realised, before she drifted off to
sleep, that she'd been awake for twenty-two hours. She'd
had to get up early on Christmas Eve to catch the train
from London to Moortown.

Her thoughts turned fleetingly to Euan. Sitting with him in the nurses' home garden had been just like old times. The emotional chemistry between them was still there. She could feel the tug of her heartstrings when she was near him. If only they could sort out their differences.

Sort them out or agree to differ, she thought as she drifted off to sleep.

Someone was touching her sleeve. She opened her eyes. Euan was looking down at her as if he'd never seen her before. She sat up and ran a hand through her tousled hair, sensing that she probably looked an awful mess.

'Any news of baby Holly?' she asked quickly.

Euan shook his head ruefully. 'Afraid not, but I rang the police just now and they're doing all they can to find her. The radio and television stations are helping as well.'

He sat down on the edge of the couch and took hold of her hand, rubbing it between his own.

'You're still cold. I came to take you to the dining room for some tea. There's nothing happening here so Fay says it would be a good time for you to take your teabreak.'

Leaning forward, he took her in his arms. She didn't resist as the pressure of his lips on hers sent her senses reeling. It was only a fleeting kiss but she could feel her heart beating madly.

'Euan, it's like it used to be…in the beginning, before all the bitter arguments about money and division of chores in the flat and starting a family and—'

'Exactly! That's because we've shelved all the problems as we're on duty. We've still got to decide if we can live in the real world together or…'

'Or go ahead with the divorce,' she prompted in a shaky voice.

'We can't make a hasty decision,' he said slowly, 'but, as I said, my circumstances have changed. I don't have to study in my off-duty times any more so theoretically I've got more time. My salary has increased to the point where I could easily afford to pay all the household bills. So…'

He was looking searchingly into her eyes.

She swallowed. 'Do you think our marriage is so fragile that it can only survive when the going is good? If we go through another bad patch will the cracks begin to show?'

'That's a risk we would have to take if we decided to give it another go.'

She looked up into his sincere grey eyes as she heard the earnestness of his tone.

He stood up, holding out his hands towards her. 'No decisions yet. It's too soon. We must give ourselves time. Come on, let's go and have some tea.'

The remains of the Christmas dinner had been cleared away from the dining room and the tables set with sandwiches, mince pies and Christmas cake. Pieces of coloured paper from the crackers they'd pulled at midnight had been collected into boxes, stacked by the door. The fairy lights on the Christmas tree shone down on the festive scene.

Carol poured out two cups of tea from the huge pot in the middle of the table and took an egg and cress sandwich from the large serving plate.

'I can never get used to having afternoon tea in the middle of the night,' Euan said, biting into a sandwich. 'Especially when I'm just about to go to bed.'

She felt a pang of emotional panic. 'Are you going off duty?'

He put down his cup and picked up the serving plate, offering it to Carol. 'Have another one of these. They're very good. Yes, I'm going off as soon as I've finished my tea. I need a couple of hours' sleep so I can stay awake when I'm on call during Christmas Day. How about you? I expect you can sleep all day if you want to.'

She forced a smile. 'I'm not going to waste the day sleeping. I'll have a couple of hours when I go off duty.'

'What are you planning to do with yourself?'

'I ought to go over to see my mother's cousin, Brenda, and her husband. They were the people I lived with after my parents died.'

'They're your only relatives, aren't they?'

'The only ones who're still alive. My parents were getting on in life when they married, you know—that's why they were so glad to produce a child. But it wasn't easy. Mum had eight miscarriages before—'

'I didn't know... You never told me.'

She could hear the genuine concern in his voice.

'Didn't I?' She hesitated. 'I didn't like to talk about it when...when I was hoping to have children of my own. Call me superstitious if you like but I was afraid if I dwelt on the subject it might happen to me. Anyway, I was really scared that if I left it too long I might have difficulties, like Mum did, and—'

She broke off as a couple of young student nurses, chattering and laughing, sat down at their table.

Euan took his hand from hers, but the expression in his eyes was tender as he said, 'I wish you'd told me...about the miscarriages, I mean.'

His voice was quiet and sympathetic. She glanced across the table. The two pale blue uniformed student nurses, deep in animated conversation, weren't interested in listening in to the drama unfolding at the other side of the table.

Carol put down her cup and leaned back in her chair. 'Would it have made any difference?'

She saw an expression of pain flit across his eyes.

'It might,' he said quietly, 'but I was hell bent on getting my fellowship and then a consultancy. All the same, I wish you'd told me because, if I'd known, I would have been able to understand what you were going through. You simply kept on about not wanting to be an older mother and, as you still hadn't reached thirty when all this started, I couldn't understand why—'

'Euan, let's not talk about it now,' she interrupted, noticing that the nurses had stopped chattering and were now straining their ears to find out what the earnest conversation was all about.

Euan's mobile phone began to ring. He took it out of his pocket. 'Yes, Fay. Be right with you.' He stood.

'I thought you were going off duty. What is it? Have they found Holly?'

He shook his head. 'No. It's a newly admitted patient in A and E. A child with breathing problems so we'd better hurry.'

She followed him out of the dining room, down the corridor and through the swing doors into A and E.

The little boy was lying on a stretcher, his face blue, gasping for breath.

'What happened?' Euan asked the distraught mother, who was hanging onto the stretcher.

'I don't know. I heard Peter go downstairs early this morning. I went down soon afterwards to tell him to go back to bed. We had a party last night and I was too tired to clear up. Peter was lying among all the mess, crying and—'

'Had he eaten or drunk anything?' Carol interrupted.

Peter's mother frowned. 'He might have drunk some of the drinks from the half-empty glasses or he could have eaten...*peanuts*!' The distraught mother screamed out the word. 'He's allergic to peanuts and there were still a few—'

'His throat's swelling,' Euan said, examining the boy's throat. 'I'm going to make an airway for him to breathe through. Come with me, Carol.'

Euan was already pushing the trolley through the door into the treatment room.

She knew exactly what Euan was going to do and why he had to act fast. It was literally a matter of life or death. The lining of the boy's throat was swelling rapidly and unless an opening was made he wouldn't survive.

She turned in the doorway and spoke to the mother in a gentle voice.

'Would you like to wait outside, please? I'll call you when the treatment is finished.'

Quickly she attracted the attention of a student nurse. 'Nurse, will you bring Peter's mother a cup of tea, please, and stay with her until we've finished treating her little boy?'

A tracheostomy operation to make an opening in the boy's throat was not the sort of treatment a worried mother should have to witness.

Euan was lifting the now-unconscious Peter onto the treatment table. She helped to position a sandbag high under the boy's shoulders so that his head was hanging over the end of the table, before reaching for the sterile emergency tracheostomy pack.

There was no time to scrub up, no time for all the usual preoperative preparations. Supporting the young boy's head over the end of the table, Carol held her breath as Euan made a swift incision in the midline, below their patient's Adam's apple. Dissecting carefully,

Euan made a hole between the third and fourth rings of the trachea, the windpipe, holding back the surrounding tissue with retractors.

'You can insert the tracheostomy tube, Carol,' Euan said.

She leaned across and carefully inserted the outer tube into the tracheal hole that Euan had made. She'd done this before, several times, but never as an emergency. She had to get it right first time. Waves of apprehension flooded over her, but passed as she successfully sited the tube.

'Good,' Euan said, removing his retractors. 'Now the inner tube, please.'

Carol slotted in the inner tube, before tying the tapes of the outer tube round the boy's neck.

A gurgling sound came through the tube.

Carol gave a sigh of relief. 'He's breathing.'

She looked down at the steady rise and fall of Peter's lungs.

'Only just in time,' Euan said, running a hand through his dark hair, which was damp with sweat.

On the surface he'd appeared calm but Carol knew he must have been as apprehensive as she had been. No, apprehensive was too mild a word. She'd been petrified that they mightn't be in time to save Peter's life.

'Thanks, Carol,' Euan said, stretching out his hand and taking hold of hers. 'Look, Peter's colour's coming back.'

She revelled in the strong grasp of his fingers as she looked down at the unconscious child.

'I'll get a porter and take Peter up to Paediatrics,' Carol said. 'Will you speak to his mother or shall I?' she added, as she picked up the phone to call for a porter.

'I'll go and explain what's happening,' he said. 'She needs to know that this is only a temporary measure until the swelling of the throat has subsided. When I've seen her I'll go and get some sleep.'

'Yes, you must be tired.'

The feeling of emotional panic was returning. Supposing she didn't see him again before she went off duty. She couldn't leave it like this...

'What time are you coming back?' she asked, her eyes searching his face for any sign of emotion.

'Why don't we have breakfast together when you go off duty? I'll meet you back here.'

'I'd like that,' she said quickly.

The door opened as the porter arrived, and she gave all her attention to her young patient.

She handed over her small patient to Sister Ann Threadgold in the children's ward, telling her that his mother would be along when Euan had reassured her. Ann stationed the suction apparatus beside Peter's bed.

'The tracheostomy tube is clear at the moment,' Carol said. 'I suctioned out the mucus that had collected in the tube from Peter's throat just before I came up here.'

She stroked the dark, damp hair from the boy's forehead.

'Poor little lamb. What a rotten thing to happen on Christmas Day. Never mind, we'll soon have you better. But I bet you won't eat peanuts again.'

'Too true!' Ann said. 'Strange isn't it, peanut allergy? Most people can eat as many as they like but there's a small unfortunate minority who can't eat even one, without having a bad reaction.'

'Apparently, Peter's mother had forgotten to clear them away after a party and Peter went down early in the morning and helped himself,' Carol said.

'I phoned you a little while ago in A and E but they said you were in the treatment room so I left a message about young Adam,' Ann said. 'You told me you wanted to know the result of his tests.'

'How is he?' Carol asked quickly.

'It's not meningitis.'

'Oh, thank God for that! What do they think it is, then?'

'A rare form of septicaemia. But the penicillin should clear it up in a few days.'

'So Euan prescribed the right treatment,' Carol said quietly.

'I was surprised Euan was still here to do this tracheostomy,' Ann said. 'I thought he would have gone off duty by now. Isn't he working on Christmas Day?'

'I believe he's on call,' Carol said, turning to go. 'I'll have a quick look at Adam and then I must be getting back.'

'How's it going, Carol?'

Carol paused, one hand on the end of the bed. 'How's what going?'

'Oh, you know…you and Euan.'

Carol drew in her breath. 'We haven't had time to discuss anything properly… I must go, Ann.'

She went into the side ward where little Adam was now sleeping peacefully. Touching his head, she could feel immediately that the fever was subsiding. She smiled as she saw one of his arms still clutching his beloved Teddy.

She had a sudden mental image of Euan, putting his stethoscope to the teddy bear's chest and pretending to listen. He was so good with children. Once again she thought how good he would have been with his own children.

As the thought crossed her mind, she felt a positive physical ache deep down inside her at what might have

been...at what still might be possible if they could re-
solve their differences.

Back in A and E she found that the department was
still quiet. Fay looked up from the report she was writing.

'How are you feeling now, Carol?'

'I'm fine. It's not long before I go off duty.'

'I got a call from Orthopaedics. They're rushed off
their feet up there and asked if I had any nurses to spare
during our quiet period. You don't have to go if—'

'I'd like to help them,' Carol said quickly.

She didn't want to wait around in A and E with Fay
poised to ask questions about Euan she couldn't answer.
And it would give her a chance to catch up with some
of the patients they'd admitted during the night. She was
particularly anxious to know how Ryan Brown, the
young Moortown footballer, was getting on after the operation on his leg.

On her way up to Orthopaedics she found herself
praying that Frank Webster hadn't had to do an amputation.

Auburn-haired Kerry Bromley, the recently appointed
sister on Orthopaedics, welcomed her to the ward. Carol
hadn't met her before.

'Bless you, Staff Nurse, another pair of hands! Would
you take over the medicine round, please?'

'Yes, Sister. Just one thing. How's Ryan Brown?'

'As well as can be expected. He's over there, bed
sixteen. I've got a nurse specialling him so she'll show
you his charts.'

Sister Bromley turned away to answer the ringing
phone.

Carol went over to bed sixteen. There was a sheet
draped over a large cage in the lower part of the bed.

She swallowed hard. What was underneath the cage, a stump or a leg?

'How's Ryan?' she asked the nurse.

'He's a much better colour now,' the nurse said, as she adjusted the flow of the intravenous blood.

'Did he...? What's his diagnosis?'

'Multiple injuries to right leg—fractured femur, tibia and fibula.'

She stared, wide-eyed, at the nurse. 'You mean they didn't amputate, in spite of the extensive injuries?'

'No, Mr Webster repaired the injuries to the tissues and put the whole leg in a long leg plaster of Paris. He'll have to operate again when the tissue repairs have settled down but there's a good chance that the leg will eventually heal.'

Relief flooded through her as she looked down at the still unconscious Ryan. She would have liked to have spoken to him. It was good to know he hadn't lost the leg.

'Thanks, Nurse,' Carol said, as she turned away, moving across the ward to begin the medicine round.

A young nurse was trundling the early morning tea trolley around as Carol was dispensing the medicines.

'Can't take my medicine till I've had my cup of tea, Staff Nurse,' called a chirpy voice.

She looked at the young man, propped against the pillows, his pristine long leg plaster sticking out from underneath an orthopaedic cradle.

She smiled as she recognised her patient, who'd come in during the early part of the evening with a fractured tibia and fibula. She and Euan had aligned the bones of his lower leg and fixed him in plaster of Paris.

'Brad Somers! You're looking better than you did last night,' she said. 'Mr Maitland has written you up for painkillers if you need them. How's the leg feeling?'

'Leg's OK. Got anything for a hangover?'

Carol remembered the alcohol fumes that had wafted over her as she and Euan had worked on the leg.

'These should help,' she said, handing Brad some painkillers.

As she went around the ward, meeting up with and chatting to some of the patients they'd admitted during the night, she was glad she'd agreed to come and work in Orthopaedics. It was a good way to end her session of night duty.

As she was finishing the medicine round, Sister Bromley came up to speak to her.

'Sister Gordon rang from A and E, asking if you could go back as soon as I can spare you. Thanks very much for your help, Staff Nurse.'

Back in A and E she found Fay, stitching a head wound on a man the paramedics had found lying in the gutter at the edge of the road.

'There's a young man with a hand wound that needs stitching, Carol,' Fay said, glancing up briefly.

Carol went into the next cubicle and was relieved to find the wound was superficial. With only six stitches, she drew the edges of the skin together.

'What happened to you?' she asked as she fixed the sutures.

'I was on my way home from a Christmas party, drinking a bottle of beer,' the young man began in a slurred voice. 'I tripped up and fell. The bleeding bottle broke. What a waste!'

Carol could hear the sound of voices in the corridor. She glanced up at the clock. The day staff were here. In a few minutes she would be free to go off duty...to have breakfast with Euan.

'That it, Nurse? Can I go now?'

She smiled at her patient. 'Is anybody with you?'

'My mate's in the waiting room. We only live just round the corner.'

'Well, mind how you go.'

She watched him walk out into the waiting room. His friend stood up and put his arm around his shoulder.

'He'll be OK with me, Nurse.'

'Take care of him.'

'Carol, it's time you were off.'

Her mind registered Fay's words and she felt a surge of excitement, tinged with sadness, that she was leaving all this behind. But she was going to have breakfast with Euan and that was all that mattered.

CHAPTER SIX

WITH mixed feelings, Carol went into Fay's office to report that she was going off duty.

Fay put down her pen and smiled. 'Are you ready?'

Carol smiled back, experiencing a mixture of relief that she would soon be able to put her feet up and sadness that she would be leaving her much-loved hospital.

'Yes. I've enjoyed being back in the old hospital again. Apart from the awful abduction of that dear little baby. Any news?'

Fay shook her head. 'I'll find it hard to sleep today, with the memory of delivering baby Holly uppermost in my mind. I'll get my mum to waken me if she hears anything on the news.'

'I hope they'll soon find her,' Carol said earnestly. 'It's always there at the back of our minds, isn't it?'

Fay nodded. 'Anyway, it's been great, having you back here. Pity you have to leave us.'

'I'm having breakfast with Euan. He's meeting me here so…'

'Have a coffee while you're waiting.' Fay reached for the kettle and a couple of mugs. 'Day Sister's taken over so we're both off duty.'

Carol kicked off her shoes and curled up in one of the two battered-looking armchairs. Fay sat opposite her in the other one.

'So you're having a breakfast meeting together—you and Euan?' Fay said, between sips of coffee.

Carol curled her hands around the mug and nodded. 'Yes.'

'Thrashing out the details of who gets what, I suppose.'

Fay's eyes were scrutinising her face. She owed it to her friend to put her in the picture. Of all her medical colleagues, Fay was the one she could really trust to keep a secret.

'Oh, we never had any joint possessions. The flat we shared was rented and furnished so when I left Euan simply gave it back to the owners. There won't be any talk about who owns what. It will all be very amicable if, in fact, we actually—'

'Well, you certainly seemed to be getting on well during the night. I almost thought that—'

'Fay, I know what you're going to say, and that's what I want as well.'

Fay's eyes widened. 'You mean...?'

The phone rang. Fay ignored it. 'You mean you're really and truly hoping to get back together again? But that would be—'

Carol reached for the phone. 'The day staff are all busy out there. I'd better... Hello, Staff Nurse Maitland speaking. Oh, it's you, Euan.'

Fay was smiling across at her. Carol uncrossed her legs and sat up straight in the chair as she listened to what Euan had to say.

'I'm sorry, I can't join you for breakfast, Carol. I'm on my way up to Paediatrics to play Father Christmas. James Haddon, our paediatrics consultant, just rang to say he isn't feeling too well this morning and asked me to stand in for him. I think he's either got flu or a hangover or both. So you go ahead and have your breakfast.'

'No, I'll wait for you. Euan, why don't I come up to Paediatrics and watch the children, opening their prezzies?'

Carol could see Fay, grinning broadly and giving her the thumbs up sign.

On the phone, Euan gave a mock groan. 'You mean, watch me making a fool of myself?'

'You'll be a wow! The children will love you.' She had to stop herself from saying that so would she.

'OK, you can come,' he said grudgingly, 'but don't get the giggles in front of the children when you see me in my long white beard.'

'Would I?'

'I've got to go, Carol.'

She heard the click of the phone at the other end.

'That's better!' Fay said. 'That's more like the old Carol I used to know. Stick to your guns and go for it, girl! You don't want this divorce any more than Euan does.'

'Euan has very strong reservations about getting back together again,' Carol said, her voice changing quickly from the bantering tone she'd adopted on the phone.

'He's bluffing!' Fay said animatedly. 'Believe me, Carol. He was like a zombie the day after you walked out on him. Oh, he was still functioning brilliantly as a doctor but you could see he was numb inside. I know that was why he left here immediately and went to work in London—so that he wouldn't be reminded of you all the time.'

Carol felt a surge of hope. 'Well, he seems to have got over it.'

'On the surface, perhaps, but... Carol, I don't know how to put this but... I didn't mean to tell you but...'

'Go on,' Carol said, intrigued by the sheepish look on Fay's face.

'Well, when I was in London in the summer... You remember I told you my mother and I bumped into Euan in Harrods? Well, I did something rather silly. I...'

Carol waited. 'What do you mean?'

'I told Euan I had two tickets for the opera and my mother didn't want to go. I asked if he'd like to go with me.'

She paused, her eyes searching Carol's face.

'And did he?'

'Yes, it was *La Boheme*.'

'Well, that's great, Fay! *La Boheme* is one of Euan's favourite operas. What's silly about that?'

'I...I didn't have any tickets when I asked him. I rushed out and bought some because I wanted to spend some time with him. I don't think he realised how I felt about him.'

Carol stared at her friend. 'How you felt about him,' she repeated, her thoughts racing ahead of her. 'And how did you feel about him?'

'I've always admired him,' Fay said slowly, one finger nervously twisting a short strand of dark hair behind her ear. 'But when I met him in London that day he looked so... Well, anyway, I convinced myself I was in love with him. And with you out of the way I thought there was no reason why I shouldn't go after him.'

Carol swallowed hard as waves of unwanted jealousy flooded through her.

'Well, you were right about that, Fay,' she managed to say, to put her friend out of her obvious discomfiture. 'I mean, we were separated. And it was only a trip to the opera.'

'If only I'd left it at that!' Fay said miserably. 'I invited him back to the hotel for a drink afterwards. Said I had some photos I wanted to show him.'

'But your mother was—'

'We'd taken a suite. She was in one of the two bedrooms fast asleep. I poured Euan a stiff Scotch—which, incidentally, he didn't drink—and then I said I was...

Oh, this sounds so corny now, but you know all those black and white films we used to giggle over where the heroine slips into something more comfortable?'

'You didn't?'

In spite of the waves of jealousy, Carol found herself giving a little giggle.

'My God, you're incredible, Carol!' Fay said, relief etched across her face. 'I'm so glad you can see the funny side of it. Believe me, it wasn't funny at the time. I made such a fool of myself.'

Carol's mouth was wide open as she stared at her friend in horror. 'You mean you started stripping off?'

'No. But I would have liked to. I started going towards the bedroom, hell-bent on returning in the new negligee I'd bought especially for the occasion that afternoon. I think Euan must have realised how I felt about him because he stood up and said he had to be going.'

'And that was it?'

Carol could feel the relief flooding through her. She'd feared the worst but it was going to be all right after all. She couldn't bear to think of Fay and Euan together.

'Not quite,' Fay said, and the sheepish look returned to her anxious face. 'I went towards him and put my hands on his shoulders, and I think I said something like, 'What's the rush? You can stay, if you like.''

Carol drew in her breath as a mental image of Fay and Euan together in the middle of the night in Fay's hotel room forced itself upon her.

'And what did Euan do?' she asked, not really wanting to know the awful details but finding it impossible to remain in ignorance.

Fay took a deep breath. 'Very calmly he removed my hands from his shoulders and told me he didn't want to spoil our friendship. He said he knew that you and I were great friends and if ever you and he got back together again he didn't want to have anything on his conscience.'

'He said that? I mean, if ever we got back together again?'

Fay nodded. 'I asked him if he thought that was likely and he said he lived in hope but that you would have to make the first move. You'd been the one who'd walked out and instigated the separation order so you would have to be the one to come back again when you were ready.'

Carol leaned back and took a deep breath. 'And then I turned up, out of the blue, on Christmas Eve, pressurising him into thinking about whether he wanted a divorce or not,' she said, in a small voice.

'Exactly! I think the poor man must have been shell-shocked. You've got to convince him you really don't want a divorce. It was all a mistake.'

Carol put out her hand and squeezed Fay's. 'Thanks for telling me about the London episode.'

'No hard feelings?'

'I must admit I felt jealous while you were telling me about it, but I'm glad you did because it's made me even more determined that—' She broke off and stood up, straightening the skirt of her uniform.

'Anyway, I'll go up and see him play Father Christmas,' she said quickly. 'I'm a big kid at heart and I love watching children opening presents.'

'Let me know how you get on. Don't keep me in suspense.'

Carol turned to look at her friend. 'I'll keep in touch. I'm glad we had our little talk, Fay. It's not going to be easy. Euan can be very stubborn.'

'Go on, you can do it!'

'I can try...but, Fay, don't talk about this to anyone, please, until...'

'You have my word,' Fay said, her face solemn and sincere.

As she went into the children's ward Carol felt a rush of excitement.

'Come into the office,' Ann said as soon as Carol pushed open the swing doors. 'I'm having trouble fixing Euan's beard. There's something wrong with it. Look, what do you think?'

Euan was sitting in front of Ann's desk, a long red coat over his grey suit, a red hood hanging down his back and a half-fixed beard dangling over the lower part of his face.

Carol put a hand over her mouth as she tried to stifle the laughter that was rising in her throat.

Euan pulled a wry face. 'I knew you'd laugh when you saw me.'

'Like I said, the children will love you,' Carol said, moving over to Ann's desk.

'I've got to go back on the ward,' Ann said. 'Can I leave the finishing touches to you, Carol? I'll come and tell you when it's a good time for Father Christmas to make his entrance.'

The door closed behind her. Carol smiled down at Euan who was still slumped in the chair. He pretended to scowl back.

'It's all right for you to look so pleased with yourself, Carol. You haven't got to go in there and say, 'Ho, ho, ho!' through a mass of cotton wool, and...'

'Your beard's too fluffy round the mouth. Look, if I snip a bit off here...'

She took the scissors from the pocket of her uniform dress, leaned forward and carefully snipped around the mouth section. As she exposed Euan's full, sensuous lips she felt the stirrings of desire deep down inside her.

Those lips that had tantalised hers so many times before...

Euan caught her by the wrist, drawing her towards him. It was as if an electric current had sprung up between them. Impatiently, he pulled the beard away from his face and pressed his lips against hers.

She gave a barely audible sigh as he pulled her onto his lap. The kiss was becoming mutually more demanding. Euan was caressing her in the way that had always roused her...but that couldn't happen here...

The door opened. Carol leapt up from Euan's lap.

Ann's eyes were twinkling as she said, 'We're ready for you now, sir.'

Euan hauled himself to his feet, pulling the beard back over his face. Carol smoothed down the crumpled skirt of her uniform dress and looked up at him.

'The beard looks better, Euan.'

He smiled down at her. 'It feels much more comfortable now.'

'Yes, it's vastly improved,' Ann said. 'What did you do to it, Carol?'

'I just made sure he could use his mouth more easily,' Carol said.

Her eyes met Euan's, and to her horror she could feel the colour, rising in her face. For the first time in years she was going to blush!

She experienced a heady feeling as she watched Euan leave the office. Ann had suggested she waited for a few seconds, before following him out, and then she was to join in with the rest of the nursing staff while she watched the proceedings.

She smiled to herself as, from outside in the corridor, she could hear Euan beginning his first, 'Ho, ho, ho!'

There was a squeal of excitement from the first child

to spot Father Christmas. Carol couldn't contain her impatience any longer!

She hurried into the ward in the wake of the awesome red-coated figure. The older children who could get out of bed were crowding around him. The younger ones hung back, waiting to see what would happen.

'Over here by the tree, children,' Euan said, in his deep, gruff, yet child-friendly voice. 'Presents by the tree.'

'Yeah! I want a present.'

'I want a present.'

'I want a new bike!'

'I want…'

Euan was lowering his sack beside the tree as he sank onto the strategically placed chair. He was on his own, surrounded by the excited children. Carol felt a wave of compassion towards him, wondering how he would cope.

Quickly she moved towards the boisterous crowd.

'One at a time, children,' she said firmly, as she stationed herself beside Euan.

Glancing down, she saw that his beard was hanging by a loose piece of sticky tape from his ears. Quickly and deftly, she secured the errant tape behind his ears.

Euan flashed her a grateful smile through the mass of cotton wool. 'Would you like to help me hand out the presents, Staff Nurse? This one is for someone called Tom.'

'That's me! I'm Tom!'

Carol handed the bulky package over the heads of the eager children to a small boy with a bandage round his head at the back.

'Wot you got?' his little friend asked.

Paper was flying in all directions as Tom tore open his present. 'It's a racing car! Brrm…brrm…'

Carol smiled as she saw the little boy zooming off around the ward.

'Edward…where's Edward?' Euan said, handing Carol another present.

'I'm here!'

'There you are, Edward.' Carol handed over the parcel.

'Happy Christmas, Edward,' Euan called.

Carol felt a lump rising in her throat as she watched Euan. She was having a happy Christmas, the happiest she'd had for three years. But what would happen when the make-believe had to stop…when they got down to decision time?

How was she to convince Euan that they could make their marriage work? Was she really sure that she could convince herself? That idyllic kiss, only minutes ago, had shown that they could still stir sensual feelings in each other, but marriage was built on more than just sexual attraction, important though it was.

Was she just being swept along by the magic of Christmas? When the tinsel on the tree was removed and the decorations stored away for another year, would she find the reality of marriage had destroyed the magic?

'This is for Deborah.' Euan was touching her arm. 'Are you OK?' he whispered.

'I'm fine! Sorry, temporary lack of concentration.'

'You're probably suffering from lack of sleep,' he said, delving once more into the capacious sack.

'Something like that.' She smiled down at the little girl who had pushed her way through the excited group, crowding around Euan. 'Are you Deborah?'

The little girl nodded shyly. 'My mummy asked Father Christmas to bring me a dolly with real hair.'

'Let me help you unwrap this…there you are! Isn't

she pretty?' Carol said, relieved that the collaboration between parents and nursing staff had worked.

Deborah, hugging the doll, was moving away to put it to sleep in her bed.

The present-giving continued. Carol carried the presents across to the children who couldn't get out of bed. Extra parcels had been prepared for the emergency admissions. She found little Michael Fieldman, the six-year-old they'd admitted during the night. He had a bandage over his injured eye and was sitting up in bed, waiting anxiously to see if Father Christmas had found out where he was.

He was delighted with the parcel that Carol gave him. His mother, sitting beside him, helped him to take the paper off the large model of a petrol station. She had arranged for it to be brought in from home.

Carol smiled down at her and whispered, 'Well done!'

Mrs Fieldman smiled back. 'The eye doctor's coming to see Michael again this morning. He doesn't think he'll have to operate.'

Carol picked up Michael's charts and studied them. Gordon Carr, the ophthalmic senior registrar, had examined him during the night and had found the functioning of the eye to be normal.

'Good,' Carol said, putting the charts back at the end of the bed. 'There's no permanent damage to Michael's eye. He's been very lucky.'

'When can I take him home, Staff Nurse?' Mrs Fieldman asked.

'You'll have to ask the doctor when he comes around this morning. I wouldn't think he'll be in long. The injured tissues should heal fairly quickly in a boy of Michael's age.'

Michael, oblivious to his surroundings, was setting out his petrol station in the middle of his bed.

'Isn't it time you went off duty, Staff Nurse?' Mrs Fieldman asked. 'You've been on duty all night, haven't you?'

Carol smiled. 'I'm off duty now—just helping out. Wouldn't miss this for anything.'

'Children make Christmas, don't they?'

Carol nodded. 'Yes, they do,' she said quietly, feeling a sudden pang of sadness sweep over her.

'I've just heard that a baby was abducted during the night. What a terrible thing to happen! The mother must be going through hell. I hope they find it soon.'

'I hope so, too,' Carol said earnestly. 'The police have got a massive search organised and the television and radio are playing a major part.'

'Let's hope they find the baby before—'

'I'd better get back to helping Father Christmas or he'll give me the sack,' Carol put in quickly, not wanting to dwell on her worst fears for baby Holly.

Euan was holding out a present for Carol to take to Adam Grayson in the side ward. She found the little boy's temperature had gone down dramatically during the night. His mother, sitting beside him, looked up at Carol and smiled.

'Such a relief to hear he hasn't got meningitis, Staff Nurse! Sister says it's septicaemia.'

'Yes, Adam's responding to treatment,' Carol said, holding the little boy's wrist so that she could feel his pulse. It was only slightly raised and he was looking much better.

'How's Teddy this morning, Adam?' Carol asked.

Adam smiled. 'He's thirsty again.'

'He's always thirsty.' Carol lifted the glass of water from the bedside table and put it to the teddy bear's mouth. 'Now your turn, Adam. That's a good boy...

Keep drinking, won't you? That will help to get you better.'

She went back to Euan, who had emptied his sack and was now chatting to a small boy who had climbed onto his lap.

'Where do you get all the toys from, Father Christmas?'

Carol waited for Euan to reply. He looked up at her as if signalling for help.

'Father Christmas gets some from the fairies and some from the mummies and some—'

'I haven't got a mummy.'

Carol swallowed the lump in her throat as she leaned forward to stroke back the hair falling over the boy's forehead.

'Have you got a daddy?' she asked gently.

'Yes, he's coming to see me today.'

Round blue eyes stared up at Carol. 'I did have a mummy but she left us.'

How could anyone leave a gorgeous little blue-eyed boy like this? she wondered. Her eyes met Euan's and she blinked back the threatened tears.

'Would you like a plane or a ship, Jimmy?' Euan was asking the little boy as he held up two bulky, brightly coloured packages.

'I'd like a plane. I've never been on a plane but my mummy has. She's gone to live with another daddy in America. She might ask me to go and stay with them,' he added doubtfully, 'but I'd rather stay with my dad. He makes really good chips and baked beans…and sausages sometimes.'

Euan was lifting the little boy from his lap, preparing to carry him over to his bed in the corner of the ward.

'Goodbye, Jimmy,' Carol said, smiling at the plucky youngster.

He was the sort of boy who would survive whatever life threw at him. She couldn't worry about all the complicated lives of her patients. She had to concentrate on straightening out her own.

'Ready?'

Euan was standing beside her, having settled Jimmy with one of the nurses, who was helping him to unwrap his Christmas plane.

She realised that she had been standing by the tree deep in thought while all around her was hustle and bustle. Her limbs felt tired but her brain was still active.

'Yes, I'm off duty,' she said. 'So, how about that breakfast you promised me?'

They walked towards Sister's office.

'Let's escape before I get roped into doing any more festive activities,' Euan said, pushing open the door.

The room was fortunately empty. Carol was relieved to see that Ann had now gone off duty and handed over to the day staff. With any luck they would escape, without having to chat to anyone.

'Help me with this wretched beard!' Euan said, clutching at the cotton-wool contraption. 'The sticky tape seems to have... Ouch.'

'Sorry!' Carol said, as she gave a final pull. 'But you know how we always tell the patients when we're removing plasters that a short sharp shock is easier than a long drawn-out situation.'

'You're a hard girl, Sister Maitland,' Euan said, and then stopped, almost in embarrassment.

'You've been calling me Staff Nurse all night,' Carol said softly. 'Why the sudden promotion?'

He shrugged off the voluminous red coat and stepped out of the wide draw-stringed trousers to reveal his pristine suit underneath.

'A slip of the tongue,' he said quietly. 'I think my

mind was flitting back to the first Christmas of our marriage, six months after our wedding, when you were still Sister Maitland.'

'Yes, I was, wasn't I?' she said dreamily. 'And I was also still enjoying being Mrs Maitland.'

He stood stock still, the bundle of red clothing still in his hands. Impatiently, he tossed it onto a chair, before putting both hands on the sides of her arms.

She could feel his fingers, gently caressing her through the thin cotton of her uniform.

He bent his head towards her, his lips hovering above hers. She could hear footsteps in the corridor. Hastily, she pulled herself away, just before the door opened and Day Sister June Grigson walked in.

'Thank you so much, Mr Maitland. I do hope you'll join us later in the day. We've got lots of festivities planned.'

'I will if I have time,' Euan said, smiling, as he eased his way out of the door, with Carol following him.

They walked side by side down the corridor. On every side, as ward doors swung open, Carol could see the excitement of Christmas Day on everyone's face, staff and patients alike.

'I wonder if breakfast will be different in the dining room today,' Carol said.

'I expect they'll push the Christmas boat out but I thought we'd have breakfast in my rooms in the residents' quarters,' Euan said in a casual tone. 'It will be too noisy in the dining room to hear ourselves speak— and we do need to talk.'

Carol drew in her breath. 'We do, indeed.'

For a brief second he squeezed her hand. They were walking past the X-ray department. Someone was coming round the corner and he let go of her hand almost immediately.

Phil Morton, Euan's senior registrar, was looking pleased with himself as he met up with them.

'Glad I've found you, sir. Would you mind if I go off for a few hours? I'll keep in touch on my mobile. My girlfriend's invited me to have Christmas lunch with her parents. It's only a couple of miles away so I could dash back if—'

'Yes, do go out for lunch. As long as we can contact you, there's no problem.'

'Where will you be today sir?' Phil's shrewd eyes were fixed on the pair of them.

'Oh, here and there,' Euan said vaguely. 'I'll keep my mobile switched on. At the moment we're going to have breakfast so I'd rather you didn't disturb me unless it's a dire emergency.'

'Of course!' Phil flashed Carol a knowing smile. 'Happy Christmas!'

Euan smiled back. 'Happy Christmas, Phil!'

They turned the corner and went through Outpatients to the stairs that led down to the medical staff quarters.

Running down the stone stairs, Carol paused for a moment by the marble bust of Alexander Fleming. How many times had she run down these stairs on her way to Euan's rooms in those far-off, heady days when she hadn't a care in the world? Those wonderful days when their love was new and fresh and they were looking forward to a lifetime together.

Looking forward to a home and family, a long life of love and laughter and…

These things were still within her grasp. She put out her hand and stroked the marble bust's cheek.

'Dear old Alex,' she whispered. 'You realised a dream when you discovered penicillin. Well, I'm going to realise my dream. I'm—'

'Are you going to stand there all day?' Euan asked

wryly, from the bottom of the stairs. 'What's the fascination with Alexander Fleming all of a sudden? He's been there for ages. You must have seen him hundreds of times.'

'I know, that's why I like him. Because he's a permanent fixture. Something solid to hang onto.'

He took hold of her hand as she reached the bottom of the stairs. For a brief second he looked down at her quizzically, as if meeting her for the first time.

As they walked along the corridor, hand in hand, towards his rooms she felt her excitement mounting.

CHAPTER SEVEN

'Wow! This is a step up from the rooms you had before,' Carol said, as she stepped inside the doorway of the large, high-ceilinged sitting room.

Range after range of leather-bound books were assembled on the oak shelves which lined one wall from floor to ceiling. The outside wall was dominated by a large casement window, draped with floor-length, dark green, velvet curtains. A brightly coloured Chinese carpet held pride of place in the centre of the room, its hand-knotted dragons chasing each other with fiery nostrils flaring. Around the carpet a cushiony sofa and chairs, flanked by oak side-tables, made an inviting group.

Euan smiled. 'One of the perks of being a consultant. This is what you get for bashing your brains out at the end of long working days and taking endless exams until you feel you'll never want to put your name on a piece of paper ever again.'

Carol felt a stab of guilt. 'Was it hard—doing the fellowship exams, I mean?'

At first he didn't reply. He closed the door behind them and moved over to the large casement window, looking down into the forecourt of the hospital.

From outside, Carol could hear an ambulance, screeching to a halt, and she found herself hoping that Euan wouldn't be called away before they'd had time to have a long, serious discussion.

When he replied to her question he was still staring down into the forecourt, his broad, muscular back towards her.

'Let's say the endless studying and preparation for the exams was difficult. I had to push myself to do it even when I was dog-tired, after working in hospital. But by the time I actually took the exams I felt confident that I'd got to grips with the subject.'

She noticed, with a pang of dismay, that his tone was deadly serious, but when he turned to face her he was smiling.

'It looks freezing cold out there. I wouldn't be surprised if we had snow.'

She sensed he was trying to lighten the mood. She moved towards him and stood, looking up into his expressive eyes.

'It would be lovely to have snow on Christmas Day,' she said quietly, her eyes scanning his face. 'Euan, I'm sorry I wasn't there...when you were taking your fellowship. I mean, as your wife, I know I should have been more supportive but—'

'Don't!'

He put a finger against her lips.

'We said no recriminations on either side,' he said slowly. 'It's all in the past. We both made mistakes. But now we must only think of the future.'

He moved away from her, crossing the thick-carpeted room with long, easy strides. She followed him into the small kitchen.

'Coffee?' He reached across the ceramic-tiled surface for a percolator and a coffee-grinder.

'Yes, please. Where do you keep your cups?'

He pointed. 'That cupboard, there. I thought it would be nice to have some freshly ground coffee after all that instant stuff we drank during the night.'

'I look on instant coffee as a medicinal necessity,' Carol said, placing two blue and white, willow pattern cups on the wooden table. 'It keeps you going while you're working. These cups are pretty.'

'A present from my mother.'

Carol swung round to look at him. 'Was she really cut up when we separated?'

'I never actually told her,' he said carefully, his voice half drowned in the noise of the coffee-grinder.

'You didn't tell her?' she said incredulously. 'But how on earth could you keep it from her?'

'I was living in London. As far as my mother is concerned, that's the end of the earth. She wouldn't dream of visiting me down there.'

'And your father?'

Euan fixed a filter paper into the Wedgwood coffee-pot and carefully poured the boiling water over the ground coffee, his tongue clamped between his teeth and an expression of concentration on his face.

'I phoned Dad one time when Mum was out. I told him you'd left me and he insisted we keep it a secret. He didn't want Mum to be upset. I only go up to Scotland about once a year and I stay in a hotel because they've only got a one-bedroom bungalow now Dad's retired. Suits me fine because I don't get asked so many questions.'

'But doesn't your mother think it's strange I'm not with you?'

He gave her a wry smile. 'You and Mum were never close, were you? Neither of you made any secret about the fact that you were chalk and cheese.'

'I tried my best but—'

'I know. I'm not criticising. Mum can be very difficult even though she means well. I've concocted this story about you having a very demanding job and she's quite happy with it.'

'And your brothers and sisters? What do they think?'

'I rarely see them. We're not a very close-knit family. They're all very busy with their own lives. There isn't time to see everybody on my flying visits. Pauline and Helen have part-time jobs, as well as looking after their children, Graham's a long-distance lorry driver and Desmond's in Malaysia, working on a building project.'

'I noticed at our wedding that you didn't seem to talk to each other very much.'

'It was the way we were brought up.' He paused, his eyes searching her face. 'Dad never showed his emotions, but when I told him you'd left me I had the distinct impression that he was holding back the tears.'

He removed the filter paper and put the lid on the coffee-pot, carrying it over to the table. She watched as he poured out a couple of cups. He'd remembered she took her filter coffee black, with no sugar.

She took a sip of her coffee, cradling the cup before facing Euan across the table.

'I'm sorry your father was upset,' she said quietly.

'He's very fond of you, and so is my mother in her own brusque non-emotional way. He asked me if there was any chance you might come back to me. I said very much doubted it. I hadn't the heart to tell him you'd slapped a two-year separation order on me. I planned to tell him at a later date when he'd recovered from the initial shock.'

'And did you?'

He shook his head. 'To be honest, I didn't like to think about it myself. It seemed so final. It certainly showed me that you were deadly serious about a divorce. Well, you were, weren't you?'

She took a deep breath as his expressive eyes roamed her face in a deeply unnerving way. 'On that Christmas Eve, yes, I was bent on ending our marriage. I'd had enough of the bickering and arguing over big projects, like moving house and starting a family, and the small everyday niggles about who did what domestic chores...'

She swallowed hard as she felt the faint pricking of tears behind her eyes. She mustn't cry now when they were actually getting to grips with the problems of their relationship.

'Hey, come on, darling.' He moved swiftly round the table to hold her shaking shoulders, lowering his face to lay his lips against her hair.

'Don't cry,' he whispered, as he handed her a large white handkerchief from the top pocket of his jacket.

'Thanks.' She dabbed the tears from her cheek. 'I don't know why I'm crying. I think it's because I can remember how awful I felt whenever I thought about how I'd started the wheels in motion to end what had been such a good marriage initially. I just used to throw myself into my work and try to forget. It was OK when I was on duty but sometimes...'

'Like when you were sitting alone on a beach in Bali?' he prompted.

She nodded.

'And I thought you were having a whale of a time on your luxury cruise ships.'

He moved back to the other side of the table, picking up his coffee-cup and taking a long drink.

'I imagined you surrounded by admiring ship's doctors and handsome young sailors, all wanting the pleasure of your company, and...'

She smiled. 'Oh, there were plenty of men, wanting the pleasure of my company, as you so delicately put it, but I held them all at arm's length. And being friendly with them wasn't like being in a relationship with someone you're in love with.'

Their eyes met across the table.

'Didn't you think you could fall in love with any of these men?'

'No.'

'Why not?'

'Because when the dust had settled after I'd walked out, I realised I was still in love with you.'

She heard his deep sigh as he reached across the table to take both her hands in his. 'So why didn't you walk right back?'

'I didn't think you would want me back after the way I'd behaved. And I thought you would probably welcome a more independent lifestyle. We hadn't spent much time together during our last few months of marriage.'

He leaned back in his chair. 'Independent lifestyle! I was up to my neck in exam preparations and a full-time job. There wasn't time for anything except work.'

'How about after your fellowship exams? When you were working in the London hospital, didn't you sometimes get together with——?'

She broke off as waves of familiar jealousy flooded her. How often had she been haunted by the thought of Euan being in another relationship? Fay had tried to reassure her that Euan wasn't like that, but...

He gave her a long, slow, tantalising smile. 'Would you be jealous if I'd started a new relationship?'

'Yes,' she said, feeling a stab of something akin to physical pain. 'I would have understood why you did it but...'

'There was plenty of opportunity but I had the same problem as you. I was still in love. But I was in love with a woman who'd walked out on me. Every time I felt like chasing after you I used to take out that piece of paper you'd asked your solicitor to send me and——'

'Don't, Euan! No more recriminations.' She hesitated. 'But simply being in love…is that enough to carry us through life together?'

'It's a good start,' he said, his voice husky with emotion. 'In fact, I think we should drink a toast.'

He got up and went over to the fridge. 'I've got a bottle of champagne.'

Her eyes widened with surprise. 'Champagne in the fridge! I don't believe it!'

He deftly removed the foil from the top of the bottle and opened out the strands of wire surrounding the cork, before easing it out.

It was obvious to Carol that he'd done this a few times in the two years they'd been apart.

'Looks as if you've had some practice, Euan. Remember the first bottle you ever opened—for the toasts at our wedding?'

He laughed as he gently removed the cork.

'What a waste it was! Half of it went on the floor and I nearly broke my wrist as the cork flew out!'

They clinked their glasses together across the table.

'Happy Christmas, Carol!' Euan's eyes were tender as he looked across at her.

She could feel a lump in her throat as she replied, 'Happy Christmas!'

'And happy birthday!'

'Thanks.'

'Two years as a bachelor is a long time,' he said quietly.

'Two years as a bachelor girl on a cruise ship wasn't as much fun as you might imagine.'

'Didn't you have marvellous meals, served up by attentive waiters, and…?'

'Oh, yes, we had all that, but it didn't compensate for what really mattered. Do you know, I sometimes found myself longing for beans on toast?'

He threw back his head and laughed. It was the deep, rumbling, boyish sound that Carol had longed to hear so often when she'd been alone without him.

'I would have thought you'd never want to eat another bean in your life,' he said, with a wry grin. 'We seemed to exist on beans on toast.'

Carol smiled back. 'Quick to assemble at the end of a long spell of duty.'

'Tasted fantastic, sitting on the floor in front of that smelly old gasfire, and—'

He stopped in mid-sentence and put down his glass. 'Oh, Carol,' he breathed, his voice tenderly husky.

She could feel a prickly sensation behind her eyes. This was more than pure nostalgia. This was a new kind of love. A gentler, kinder, more caring love.

She watched as he stood and came round to her side of the table. She held her breath as he leaned down towards her, and in that moment she realised how desperately she'd missed him. It had been so long since she'd abandoned herself in his arms.

He pulled her to her feet. She felt as limp as a rag doll as his arms enclosed her in a deeply passionate embrace. She gave a moan of desire as his lips touched hers, very gently at first and then with a desperate, hungrily demanding desire.

The sound of the mobile phone's insistent ring forced itself upon her consciousness. She felt Euan pull himself away, cursing as he barked into the mouthpiece, 'Maitland!'

He was listening now, one hand running through his dark, rumpled hair. His eyes, still on her face, seemed to be pleading with her to remain in their new-found ambience of true love.

But as she watched him she saw he was shifting into

his work mode, assuming his consultant voice and concentrating on what the caller was saying to him.

He was frowning now. 'I'll be with you as quickly as I can, Sister.'

He put down the phone and held out both hands towards her. 'I've got to go back to A and E. They're bringing in an unconscious patient in an ambulance. Jill Watson thinks it could be a cardiac arrest so I need to be there when he arrives. Wait here for me, Carol.'

'I'm not going anywhere,' Carol said quietly.

He dropped a kiss on the tip of her nose. It was one of the absent-minded things he used to do in the early days when he was rushing off somewhere, one of the simple yet sensuous gestures that made her love him all the more.

'Help yourself to champagne,' he said, ramming the mobile in the pocket of his jacket. 'Mustn't waste a good bottle like that.'

He gave her a wry, teasing smile and she knew he was making fun of himself.

That's a good sign, she thought as she watched him dash out of the door. She'd teased him in the early days about his obsession with using up every scrap of food, and her remarks hadn't always been welcome. During the last six months of their time together he'd taken every remark she'd made with a deadly seriousness that had alarmed her.

She realised now that he'd been overwhelmed with work and responsibility. In pursuing his dream, he'd forgotten how to laugh and love.

Going into the sitting room, she heard an ambulance arrive on the forecourt. She looked out of the window. Way below her, Euan was hurrying outside, flanked by small, plump Jill Watson. The doors of the ambulance were opening and the paramedics were lifting out a stretcher. She caught a glimpse of a prone figure wrapped in blankets.

Euan would revive him if anyone could.

She walked through the open door at the side of the sitting room. There was a small passage, a bathroom on one side and the bedroom on the other. The king-size bed with its white, cotton-covered, fluffy duvet looked infinitely inviting.

She was so tired! She kicked off her shoes and climbed into the bed, shrugging out of her uniform dress under the soft duvet and tossing it on the floor.

Her mind flew back in time, remembering the first night of their honeymoon. They'd spent two idyllic days and nights in a farmhouse bed and breakfast on the edge of the Yorkshire moors near the sea. It had been cheap and cheerful but she remembered it as one of the most wonderful weekends of her life.

Euan had mixed just the right amount of tenderness with dynamic, virile passion. She shivered under the duvet as the memories flooded back. It could be like that again…it could…

Carol's eyes were heavy and her body felt leaden. She was falling into a deep sleep but she must keep awake for when Euan got back…

She sensed she wasn't alone, but as she opened her eyes all she could see at first was the white ceiling. A ceramic light shade was suspended above her but the light wasn't switched on.

Of course it wasn't because daylight was flooding in through the windows.

Where on earth was she? She began to sit up among the soft fluffy pillows and then she saw him.

He was sitting in an armchair at one end of the room.

A pale ray of winter sunlight was shining on his face and she felt a warm rush of desire suffusing through her.

He stood up and came towards the bed. 'I didn't mean to waken you.'

'How long have you been sitting there?'

He smiled. 'Long enough to realise that the only thing I want to do now is climb in there with you.'

She pulled back the duvet and waited as he shrugged out of his clothes, dropping them on the carpet beside the bed. She saw that his limbs and chest were still lightly tanned from the long hot summer that everyone in England had enjoyed that year.

Her own skin was tanned from her recent spell of duty in the Far East on the cruise ship. She noticed how the muscles of his upper arms stood out and how his muscular legs still gave the impression he was a professional athlete.

He'd always made time to keep himself in shape. Even when he'd spent a long day in hospital, followed by hours of studying, he would still get up early two or three times a week and run over the moors.

She moved to the middle of the bed as he climbed in beside her. Gently he pulled her against him. His hands caressed her face, slowly moving down over her shoulders, then tantalising her breasts.

'Carol, darling,' he whispered. 'Am I dreaming? Is it really you?'

She wanted to reassure him, but his sensuous lips silenced her reply.

Her senses heightened, she found it difficult to contain her impatient need for fulfilment. Deep inside she was aching for the moment when they would fuse together and become one.

Shivers of sensual excitement ran down her spine and

when at last she felt him thrust deeper and deeper inside her she gave out a long, slow moan of ecstasy.

She experienced wave after wave of climactic sensations as she clung to him. They seemed to have floated away out of this world. Nothing was real except the feeling of their bodies entwined together in this heavenly embrace...

She lay back against the pillows, panting. Running a hand through her hair, she found it was damp with perspiration. The headband, holding up her hairdo, had long since vanished. It was probably on the floor but she didn't care where it was.

She didn't care about anything except that Euan was here beside her.

He pulled her towards him again. His body was soaked in sweat. She put her head on his chest and laughed as she felt the further dampening of her hair.

He stroked her hair.

'I prefer your hair all mussed up like this,' he said in a dreamy voice. 'You looked too artificial before. Not like the Carol I remember.'

'It was supposed to make me look sophisticated for all my well-heeled patients on the cruise ship.'

'When are you due back?' he asked evenly.

She pulled away and sat up. Why wasn't he begging her to stay?

'New Year's Eve,' she said quietly. 'But, Euan...'

'Yes?'

'What are your plans for New Year's Eve?'

He pulled her back into the circle of his arms. 'The last two years I've done the dutiful trek north to see the parents, but this year...'

He paused and she waited, her heart beating rapidly. She sensed they were both waiting for the other to make the first move, to express the thoughts uppermost in their minds.

'Euan, I honestly don't think I can go back to the life I've been leading during the last two years. Not after—'

'Carol, you have to be sure,' he interrupted earnestly. 'Just because we've had a wonderful time in bed together, it doesn't mean—'

'It's not just the fact that we've made love,' she burst out heatedly.

The persistent ringing of Euan's mobile intruded on her words.

She pulled herself away and lay back against the pillows. Her physical longing for Euan had been satisfied but mentally she was totally frustrated. Every time she felt she was getting her ideas across there was some kind of interruption.

Euan had climbed off the bed and wrapped himself in a green and blue striped towelling dressing-gown. He was speaking quietly into the phone, sitting once more in the armchair at the end of the room. She saw him frown and thought, Here we go again! Another emergency! Goodbye, Euan!

He walked back to the bed, holding out the mobile towards her.

'It's for you, Carol.'

'But nobody knows I'm here,' she muttered as she took the phone.

'It's the hospital switchboard,' he explained quickly. 'They asked if I knew where you were.'

'Hello, is that Staff Nurse Maitland?' the switchboard voice enquired. 'Hold the line, I've got a call for you.'

Carol waited. The line was indistinct. Someone was speaking too quietly for her to hear.

'Could you speak up, please?' she said.

'Carol, do you remember me?' someone said, still very quietly.

'I don't recognise your voice,' Carol said, feeling a surge of impatience. If this was one of those telephone freaks...

'It's me, Penny...Penny Slater.'

She felt a frisson of horror run down her spine. It was the bogus nurse who'd stolen baby Holly.

'Hello, Penny,' she said, surprised at how normal her voice sounded, considering the pounding of her heart.

'I saw you when I was in Accident and Emergency last night,' the voice continued in a dead tone. 'You were coming out of the cubicle that I was going into. I recognised you even though your hair's darker than it used to be.'

'You were collecting a baby to take up to Obstetrics, weren't you, Penny?' Carol said, waving madly to alert Euan.

As if anticipating Carol's intentions, Penny Slater said, 'You won't be able to trace this call because I'm using my mobile and I've withheld my number. I want some advice from you, Carol.'

'The only advice I can give you is to bring back baby Holly,' Carol said evenly. 'She had a slight touch of neonatal jaundice and she may need hospital treatment so—'

'That's why I'm ringing you.' It was the same dead tone, devoid of emotion. 'It's getting worse. I knew I could trust you, seeing as we were neighbours when we were young.'

'If the baby's condition is worsening, you must bring her back at once, Penny,' Carol said, with what she hoped was the right amount of gentle firmness.

She didn't want Penny to get scared and ring off.

'Please, think of what the poor mother is going through and—'

'I can't bring her back.'

A chill hand grasped at Carol's heart.

'What do you mean, you can't bring her back?'

Euan had put his arm round her shoulders. She leaned against him.

'I daren't. They'll arrest me and put me in prison again.'

Carol was thinking on her feet. 'Then I'll come to you, Penny. Tell me where you are and I'll collect the baby from you.'

Euan's hands, firmly holding her quivering shoulders, were giving her strength.

'Come on your own, Carol. If you tell the police you won't get the baby back. I'll do something to the baby if—'

'I won't tell the police! Just tell me where you'll be.'

'I'm going to the stream in the secret valley where we used to play when we were kids. Not the main river—the stream, near the waterfall. I won't say anything else in case somebody's listening in. Remember, come on your own or else there'll be no baby.'

'Penny, wait…'

The line went dead. Carol realised she was trembling all over now. Euan was holding her against him, trying to soothe away her tension.

She took a deep breath to try to steady her nerves. 'Did you hear all that?'

'Most of it. I gather Penny Slater wants you to collect the baby from somewhere. Did you get all the details?'

'I think I know where she means. It's a long time since I went up there. I hope I can find it. She said no police or she'll harm the baby.'

'She sounds frighteningly unstable, to say the least. When you were kids together, was she normal?'

Carol thought hard. 'They were an unusual family. Cousin Brenda didn't like them. I remember Penny used to be highly strung. She easily lost her temper.'

Euan rose, a determined expression on his face.

'I'll come with you.'

'Penny said I should come alone or—'

'I'm not letting you go out to meet a potential maniac on your own. I think we should tell the police.'

'No! She'll harm the baby.'

'She could be bluffing.'

'Whether she's bluffing or not, we can't take that chance,' Carol said quickly. 'She's been in prison and she doesn't intend to go back. She sounded desperate, desperate enough to do anything. Her mind is definitely highly disturbed.'

'OK, no police, but I'm coming with you.'

CHAPTER EIGHT

THE snow started falling as they were driving away from the hospital forecourt.

Euan had spent a couple minutes briefing his housemen, Rod Grant and Geoff Bailey, about contacting him on his mobile only for a dire emergency. In any other situation they felt they couldn't handle they were to either call Phil Morton back from his girlfriend's parents' house or get help from a senior doctor in hospital from the relevant firm, surgical, medical, orthopaedics or obstetrics.

Carol had waited for Euan in the car, the heater blowing up the windscreen to defrost the opaque curtain of ice. It had only been a couple of minutes but her anxiety about baby Holly was increasing by the second. She was relieved when they finally drove away.

'Where did you tell Sister Watson you were going?' Carol asked, as Euan waited behind an ambulance, before pulling out into the main road that led to the Moortown bypass.

'I didn't,' he said as he adjusted the driving mirror, the serious tone of his voice revealing that he, too, was worried about the baby.

'Rod and Geoff are a reliable pair of doctors. They've both been asleep since midnight so they're bright-eyed and bushy-tailed this morning. Although they haven't had a lot of accident and emergency experience, they'll know if they need to call in senior medical help.'

Momentarily, he took one hand from the wheel and squeezed Carol's.

'You feel cold. Are you sure you're going to be warm enough in your uniform?'

She pulled the cloak more tightly around her. 'I'm fine. I wanted to wear uniform. I think Penny may find it easier to hand the baby over if she knows I'm going to take her straight back to the hospital. I don't want her to have a last-minute change of heart.'

Euan pulled up at traffic lights. 'Which way, Carol?'

'Straight on to the next set of lights, then turn right onto the moorland road. I'll direct you when we get up there.'

Once they got up on the moorland road they found the falling snow was making driving conditions hazardous. Euan slowed his pace.

'It's further than I thought. A long way for Penny to bring a newborn baby,' he said anxiously.

Carol frowned. 'That's what I was thinking. I suppose she wanted somewhere away from the town where the police wouldn't be looking for her.'

Euan was peering through the windscreen at the falling snow. 'She must have a car but I can't see any other tracks.'

'Perhaps she got here before the snow started,' Carol said. 'I hope she's keeping Holly warm.'

She wriggled her cold toes inside the black, slip-on shoes as she tried to improve her circulation. The navy blue regulation cardigan, worn over her royal blue uniform dress, was comfortingly large. She pulled it down over her hands, stretching them towards the warm stream of air, flowing out of the heater.

They were driving along slowly, high above Cragdale, the valley where she'd lived as a child. She looked down over the white hillside, her eyes searching through the falling snow for the house that had been home in those early years.

'Can you see the house where you were born?' Euan asked. 'I remember you showed it to me once.'

'It's down there somewhere, but I can't see through the snow. And Brenda's house is close by, remember?'

He nodded, his eyes still on the road, the windscreen wipers pushing back the snow as quickly as it fell. 'Yes, I remember going to Brenda's house once or twice. Not a very outgoing couple, Brenda and her husband, I found.'

'Well, they're very reserved. It was good of them to take me in after my parents died, but I often felt that I wasn't wanted. They had no children of their own, having married late in life, like my parents, and I think I was a bit of an imposition on them. Anyway, they did their duty towards me, but I must say it was a relief when I was old enough to escape to the nurses' home.'

'Escape?' he said wryly. 'I would have thought you were only changing one constraining situation for another set of rules, weren't you?'

'Not at all! I loved being in the nurses' home—being part of a young community, having other girls of my own age around. All that fun and activity! Yes, I felt I'd finally escaped. You've no idea how I used to hate being an only child of older parents—'

She broke off and pointed.

'There's a little track where the road curves round,' she told him, sitting up and leaning forward to peer through the windscreen. 'It's not marked so go very slowly so that... Here it is! On the left...there!'

Euan had slowed almost to a halt. 'I would never have known it was there,' he said, as he turned the wheel.

'Exactly! Penny must have chosen this place because it's so difficult to find.'

Anxiety was gnawing inside her. She remembered this track so well from childhood. It had always been exciting to spend a couple of hours away from home. A group of friends would walk up here together and bring a picnic. They'd never told their parents how far they'd be going, and in those days it hadn't seemed to matter.

Euan was driving the car slowly down the bumpy track. Carol stared out of the side window at the rough moorland, now completely white. The snow had stopped, she noticed, but the white Christmas was assured.

In front of the car a couple of sheep scattered from the track and ran up the side of the hill, bleating loudly, their noses twitching in the frosty air.

The track twisted out of sight of the main road and ended by a wooden gate.

Euan frowned. 'Now what?'

Carol opened the passenger door. 'Penny must have gone through here. The stream's down there—look!'

She climbed out of the car and pointed to the steep incline. And then she saw it—a small blue car, parked near the stream.

The rope on the gate had been left untied. Carol held the gate open for Euan to drive through, closing it after him and retying the gate. She didn't want the sheep to go through. Emergency or not, she would keep to the country code that she'd learned as a child.

'Turn your engine off and wait here, Euan,' she said quietly. 'I'll take this path down to the stream. When you see me holding baby Holly you can come down, but not before. Penny insisted I came alone or she'd harm the baby.'

'I'll be watching out for you,' he said grimly. 'Don't take any chances.'

He leaned forward and kissed the tip of her nose.

It was only yards down a short cut path to the stream. Carol could hardly contain herself as she walked the last few paces. She could hear the steady burble of the stream as it fell over the small waterfall where they'd played as children. As she got nearer she could hear something else above the noise of the water.

The sound of a baby, crying!

Oh, God! Please let her be unharmed...

Her feet slithered from beneath her and she sat down in the snow. Brushing the flakes from her cloak, she pulled herself up and ran the last few yards across the snow-covered, bumpy ground to the blue car.

With trembling fingers she wiped away the snow from one of the side windows.

Inside on the back seat was a navy blue carry-cot with a hood. It was impossible to see inside, but she could hear the wailing of the baby.

The car door wasn't locked. She wrenched it open and leaned inside. With one hand she gently pulled back the top of the white blanket. The small face under the carry-cot hood puckered into a louder cry.

'Holly,' Carol breathed, climbing in and reaching down inside the carry-cot. 'Oh, Holly, thank God you're safe!'

The small form felt reassuringly warm. The baby was dressed in a white Babygro that covered her from shoulders to tiny feet. The alarming factor that Carol noticed was the yellow colour of her skin. But, she told herself, it wasn't life-threatening if she could get Holly back to hospital as soon as possible and start treatment.

Before leaving the hospital, she'd checked on Holly's parents' blood groups. She was relieved to find they were both rhesus positive so the jaundice wasn't the more serious kind caused by rhesus incompatibility.

No, this was caused by the normal breakdown of red blood cells, which occurs in all babies after birth. If the rate of breakdown is greater than the rate of elimination the baby appears jaundiced.

Holly needed phototherapy treatment—putting the baby under a special blue light would help to cure the condition.

But where was Penny?

Suddenly Euan arrived and leaned in through the door of the car. 'I saw you'd got Holly so I came down. Is she OK?'

'Apart from neonatal jaundice,' Carol said quickly. 'We need to get her back and put her under the blue lamp so that—'

'There's someone in the stream,' Euan said, his voice grim. 'It must be Penny. I'll do what I can to save her but I don't hold out much hope. She's showing no sign of life. Keep this door closed and conserve what heat you can.'

Carol felt as if a cold hand was clutching at her heart as, through the windscreen, she watched Euan approach the stream. In her haste to get to the baby she hadn't noticed what appeared to be a bundle of clothes, floating on the top of the water. Arms outstretched, face downwards, she could see it was a body, a seemingly lifeless body.

As she held the little baby inside her cloak against the warmth of her body she found herself praying that they would be able to revive Penny. She couldn't have been there long.

How long had it been since the phone call? Half an hour? Three quarters of an hour at the most? She watched as Euan took off his anorak and shoes and waded through the snow-covered bulrushes. He was approaching the place where the bottom of the stream shelved off near the waterfall. She held her breath as she saw him plunge forward, imagining the icy impact of the water as he swam, fully clothed, towards Penny's motionless form.

She held her breath as she watched. He was now taking hold of Penny. He was supporting her with his hands under the armpits and pulled her over onto her back, before swimming back to the shore.

Baby Holly had stopped crying and had fallen into an exhausted sleep. Gently Carol placed her back in the cot, covering her as far as her shoulders with the blanket.

She slipped out of the car and ran to the side of the stream. Euan was now carrying Penny in his arms, struggling up the bank to lay her down on the snow at the top.

Carol looked at the grey, lifeless face. Could they revive her or was it too late?

Euan, shivering with the cold of the icy water, turned Penny on her side in the recovery position. As he did so, a gush of foam-like froth emptied itself onto the snowy ground.

Carol knelt down, checking that there was now a free airway to the lungs, and commenced mouth-to-mouth resuscitation. A minute passed—no sign of life. She leaned back on her heels and took a deep breath.

Euan took over. Several seconds passed and then, unbelievably, came a gurgling, coughing sound. Euan raised his head, pulled Penny onto her back and brought the heel of his hand firmly down in the middle of her chest, applying rhythmic cardiac massage as he tried to stimulate the heart.

'I can feel a pulse!' Carol said excitedly. 'Keep going, she's—'

Penny's eyes fluttered open. Carol leaned over her, one hand cradling her head.

'Penny, can you hear me?'

Penny gave a groan. 'Why?'

Her voice was faint and indistinct, but Carol could make out the plaintive words.

'Why didn't you let me go? I don't want to live any more. You should have let me die.'

Penny was struggling to sit up. Euan gently restrained her.

'Keep still, Penny. I'm going to carry you to my car. We'll soon have you in a nice warm hospital bed and then—'

'Please don't take me back there. I couldn't face...'

Euan hauled Penny up into his arms. Carol was relieved that Penny, although tall, was thin and lightweight because Euan looked exhausted. Water dripped from his hair and his suit.

'Would you like me to drive?' she asked.

'No, you take care of the patients,' he said, between his chattering teeth.

Penny was now stretched out on the back seat, her eyes closed. Carol held the baby close against her. There was nowhere else to sit with Holly, except the front seat. Not a good idea under normal circumstances but this was, after all, an emergency. The sooner they got back to hospital the better.

The wheels of the car spun a few times before Euan could get a grip on the snowy track. Slowly they climbed out of the valley and up onto the moorland road, startling the same sheep who were still nuzzling through the snow, intent on finding some grass.

Holly was still sleeping as they drove down towards Moortown. Carol heard Penny stirring on the back seat. She had put her cloak over her to try to get some warmth back into her frozen limbs. The heater was blasting forth from the front of the car and Carol could feel herself thawing out.

She glanced sideways at Euan. 'Are you OK?' she asked quietly.

He managed a wry grin. 'I've never driven in a wet suit before. Quite an experience! What I wouldn't give for a hot bath!'

'I'm sure that can be arranged when we get back,' Carol said quietly.

'Only if you'll join me,' he whispered under his breath.

She smiled, holding the baby closer to her.

They drove in through the hospital gates. Euan had already telephoned ahead to alert his housemen, who now appeared through the main door.

Stretchers were brought to the car. Carol insisted on carrying baby Holly into hospital herself. She felt almost reluctant to hand her over to Sister Galloway, the Day Sister from Obstetrics, who was already waiting in A and E to take her back to her department.

'You'll start phototherapy treatment for the jaundice immediately, won't you, Sister?' Carol said, as she handed over the precious bundle. 'And she's going to need extra fluids to help overcome her jaundiced condition.'

Patricia Galloway smiled. 'Don't worry. I'll take special charge of Holly myself. And one of our obstetrics consultants is on his way over.'

'Have you told Holly's mother she's been found?'

Sister Galloway shook her head. 'Not yet. We wanted to be absolutely sure she really was coming back before we broke the good news.'

Carol watched wistfully, a lump in her throat, as Holly was taken away down the corridor.

Euan touched her arm. 'You really love babies, don't you?' he said quietly, his eyes expressively tender. 'Watching you holding baby Holly just now, I realised just how much you've been yearning to have a baby of your own.'

Their eyes met. The light touch of his fingers on her arm was very reassuring. Was her dream of having Euan's children really going to become reality some time in the not too distant future?

Time seemed to stand still as they looked at each other in the middle of the busy department, oblivious of their surroundings.

Suddenly their poignant moment was shattered by a loud cry.

'Carol!'

The plaintive voice came from the stretcher, being wheeled towards her.

'Penny wants to have a private word with you before we take her up to the ward,' Sister Watson said. 'Let's go into my office so that nobody else will hear.'

Euan was nodding in agreement. 'You'd better see Penny by yourself, Carol, if that's what she wants. I'll give you a few minutes together before I come in to arrange some treatment for her.'

'You ought to go and get out of those wet clothes,' Carol said.

He shook his head. 'Later. I've got Penny's treatment to organise first.'

Penny's stretcher was being wheeled into Sister's office. Carol hurried after it.

As the door closed behind them, Penny reached out and touched Carol's arm, her sad eyes wide with fear.

'Don't let them put me back in prison or I'll do myself in,' she said quietly. 'I really will and this time...'

Carol squeezed her hand. 'Penny, nobody is going to put you in prison. You need help. We'll need to find out why you took Holly, of course, but—'

'I wanted a baby,' Penny said forcefully. 'And I'm

'sterile. I had an abortion that went wrong when I was fifteen. Last year I got a new boyfriend but he's married. He loves kids. I thought if I could have a baby he would leave his wife for me. So I told him I was pregnant. I said it was his.'

Carol felt the clinging pressure of Penny's hand increase. She felt a deep sadness envelop her as she looked down at the agonised expression on Penny's face.

'I haven't seen him since last summer. He's in the army in Germany. I told him the baby was due at Christmas. I've been a patient in a psychiatric hospital for the last few weeks but I kept thinking I'd have to do something about getting a baby.'

She let out a long sigh. Carol waited.

'I remembered I still had the papers my brother fixed me up with when I wanted to get a nursing job in London. But I hadn't thought it through.'

Penny was frowning, running a thin hand through her wet blonde hair. 'I sometimes have trouble thinking, Carol. Everything gets muddled. That's when they always put me back in hospital—or prison, if I've done something they don't like.'

The door opened. Euan was coming in with a man Carol recognised from way back. She knew he was a consultant psychiatrist.

He smiled down at Penny. She looked up at him quizzically.

'Who are you?'

'My name's Hugh Farmer, Penny. I'd like to help you.'

Euan signalled to Carol from the door. It was time to leave her patient.

Carol squeezed Penny's hand. 'I've got to go now, Penny, but try not to worry—you're in good hands.'

'Hugh Farmer will know how to handle this,' Euan

said, as he steered Carol out through the door. 'We can leave him to it.'

There were a few enquiring glances as they went along the corridor towards the stairs that led to the residents' quarters.

'Went for a Christmas morning swim and forgot my swimming trunks,' Euan quipped in reply to one enquiry from a stunned radiographer outside X-Ray.

'Obviously, the news about baby Holly hasn't filtered through yet,' Carol said, as they started to descend the stone staircase together.

'It will,' Euan said evenly. 'I asked my team to hold off giving news to the press until we'd got our patients settled in hospital. I expect all hell will be let loose once the press get hold of it. I've told them I'm not available for the next hour but after that I'll hold a press conference.'

'You'll be lucky if they leave you alone for an hour!' Carol said, as they passed the marble bust of Alexander Fleming.

Euan took hold of her hand. 'We deserve an hour's break so I've turned off the mobile and told the switchboard to hold all calls to my room. I need to get out of these clothes and have a bath. We'll emerge in an hour's time, ready to face the press and the cameras, and not before.'

'What luxury! A whole hour to take a bath!' Carol said.

Euan put a hand around her waist. 'Believe me, it won't be long enough.'

Carol lay back against Euan's chest with her head on his shoulder in the huge, old-fashioned bath. His arms encircled her and they lay together, spoon fashion, as they always had in that far-off former life.

Strange, how easy it had been to adopt the same positions they'd worked out so long ago.

The bath in their tiny flat had been a minuscule plastic affair, she remembered. They'd discovered how to cram themselves in like contortionists. But this enormous bath was positively palatial. Sheer luxury!

She flicked a piece of foam onto his hair. He laughed and flicked some across her shoulders. She rolled over to face him.

'Long time since we had a bath together.' His voice was husky, gravelly almost.

She sighed. 'Long time since we did anything together. Even before I left we'd stopped communicating, hadn't we?'

A worried expression flitted momentarily across his face. 'I didn't know how to approach you. You were so…so remote.'

'That was because I didn't know how to handle you. I was tired of the arguments about buying a house and starting a family. I couldn't see how to bring you round to my point of view and—'

'But that was it! You were trying to bring me round to your point of view when what we needed was a joint decision on it.'

'Euan, I was trying to convince you that you were wrong in holding out like that. When you moved into the spare room I thought my heart would break. Why didn't—?'

'I know it was a drastic step but I was desperate.'

He leaned his head against the back of the bath, his eyes staring up at the ceiling.

'I've never told you this,' he said quietly. 'When I was at medical school I had a friend called Mark who was as impoverished as I was. During term time we both had jobs in a pub, serving behind the bar, washing up—

all very menial and low paid but it helped with the practically non-existent finances.'

Carol remained quiet as she saw Euan's haunted expression and recognised that he was vividly reliving the past.

'In the holidays we used to work on a building site. Anyway, Mark had a girlfriend, a nurse called Phoebe, who went and got herself pregnant and—'

'She must have had some help from Mark,' Carol put in wryly. 'Why do men always assume it's the girl's fault if—?'

'On this occasion it *was* her fault,' Euan said firmly. 'Phoebe had told Mark she was on the Pill.'

'Ah, I see. And she wasn't?'

'She'd secretly stopped taking the Pill because she wanted to have Mark's baby.'

'But I thought you said Mark was as impoverished as you were. Surely…?'

She stopped in embarassment.

'Exactly!' Euan said. 'I rest my case.'

Carol rolled onto her back again, splashing some water over the sides of the bath. Euan's arms tightened around her.

'But I was still on the Pill, Euan!'

'Yes, but there was nothing to stop you forgetting to take it. I knew you were as desperate as Phoebe had been to have a baby. I had to be sure. Believe me, that last six months was torture, knowing you were in the next room. I'd suggested other forms of contraception, if you remember, and you'd turned the idea down.'

'I do remember,' she said slowly, 'but I couldn't see the need when the Pill was so convenient to take.'

'And so convenient not to take as well! Poor Mark was devastated when Phoebe told him she was pregnant. She carried on with her nursing training as long as she could, but she had to give up just before the baby was born.'

'And Mark?' She lifted her head from his shoulder to look enquiringly into his eyes.

He moved her gently to one side as he leaned forward to grasp the taps in the middle of the bath, topping up with hot water and swirling in some more foam from a scented green bottle.

For an instant Carol's attention wavered as she looked at the familiar green bottle.

'Wasn't that the bottle we had in the flat?'

He gave her a wry smile. 'I put it away in a box with a few other mementoes from our marriage. I got it out just now when you weren't looking.'

'I've never thought of you as being sentimental,' she said quietly. 'Go on, tell me what happened to Mark.'

'Mark moved out of the medics' quarters and rented a bedsitter way out of town. They got married after the baby was born. He was terribly hard up but he struggled on with the responsibilities of wife, son and exams to pass. During his third year he threw in the towel and left medical school.'

He pursed his lips as the memories flooded back. 'I've never seen such a change in anyone. From being a carefree young medical student, he became a bad-tempered, worried-looking man, and Phoebe looked old beyond her years on the odd occasion when I saw them together.'

'So, what you're trying to say is that you didn't want that to happen to us,' she said.

'Exactly!' He tightened his arms around her. 'I wanted to give you everything, Carol, home, family, security…'

She revelled in the feeling of his hands, caressing her breasts, and a shiver of anticipation ran through her.

He was smiling as his sensuous lips closed over hers.

A rush of foamy water splashed over the side of the bath and splattered onto the thick carpet.

Euan pulled himself away, laughing. 'It may be a huge bath but we'd be more comfortable in bed.'

He stood and reached for the fluffy towels they'd dropped on the carpet, wrapping one round her with a caressing movement.

She felt the strong stirring of desire deep down inside her as he scooped her up into his arms and carried her across the dampened carpet towards the bedroom. Her skin was still moist as he laid her on the bed. He reached down and took her face in his hands.

'I love you so much,' he murmured.

'And I love you, too,' she whispered back, as tears of happiness threatened to spill out of her eyes.

Was it possible that their hostile two-year separation was over? Making love was always wonderful with Euan, but when it all finished could they get back together again permanently?

She banished her niggling doubts as Euan's hard chest pressed against her breasts. His hands moved to caress her, gently at first and then with a virile urgency. Her skin felt as if it were on fire. Waves of sensual passion were sweeping over her as she gave herself entirely to their love-making...

As she clung to him a little while later, still feeling the climactic waves shuddering through her entire body, she reflected that their love-making had taken on a new dimension. Although it had been wildly ecstatic, there was a newfound tenderness—some extra ingredient born from the painful experience of separation.

They had to stay together!

She disentangled herself from Euan's arms and lay back with her head on the pillow, her mind working madly to form the right words that would convince him.

She turned to look at him. He was eyeing her tenderly but with a certain wariness, as if waiting for her to announce that she was about to leave.

'I can see now why you were holding off, having a family,' she said quietly. 'Your experiences as a child in an impoverished family, coupled with seeing the disaster of Mark's and Phoebe's premature launch into parenthood, were enough to—'

'I haven't told you the full story about them,' he cut in, running his hand under her shoulders and pulling her back into the cradle of his arms.

'Soon after you left me, when I was working in London, I bumped into Mark and Phoebe in a West End cinema. They invited me back to their place for supper.'

'And were they still in a bedsit?'

Euan gave a wry smile. 'No, they weren't. That was years ago, remember? They've moved on...and how! They've now got a five-bedroom house in Hampstead and—'

'But I thought you said Mark had dropped out of medical school.'

'He did. But you can't keep a good man down. After working on building sites for a while, he'd borrowed some money and started his own company, eventually employing a large work force and going into property development. He told me it had been a lot of hard work but he didn't regret doing it all for his wife and children.'

She felt a pang of unwelcome jealousy. 'How many children have they got?'

'Four—two boys and two girls. Lovely kids they are.'

He took a deep breath. 'It set me thinking. I decided that perhaps I'd been wrong to make us wait like that and...'

She pulled a wry face. '*Perhaps* you'd been wrong?' she queried wryly.

He smiled. 'OK...yes, I was wrong. I expect we'd have made out whatever happened.'

'I'm sure we would. But I would never have pulled the wool over your eyes, Euan. I wouldn't have skipped taking the Pill.'

'I know that now. I'm sorry I doubted you, but I knew that some women will go to any lengths to have a baby.'

'You're right there,' Carol said, a wave of sadness sweeping over her as she thought of poor, misguided Penny.

'I'm sorry that I couldn't understand your point of view,' she said carefully.

He rolled on his side and propped himself up on his elbow, his eyes tenderly searching her face. 'There's an old saying that love means never having to say you're sorry.'

'We've both said we're sorry,' she said quietly. 'We've cleared the air. Do you think we can move on from here?'

'You mean call a halt to the divorce proceedings?' he said, his voice suddenly serious.

She swallowed hard. 'Yes.'

He pulled her against him. 'I never wanted a divorce in the first place. It was entirely your idea. You've got to be sure, Carol. I couldn't bear it if you walked out again.'

He was caressing the side of her cheek with smooth, gentle, loving movements.

His eyes held a veiled expression. 'It's been wonderful to be together again, but we've got to be sure. Better to go through with the divorce than risk another—'

'Euan, I want us to stay together for the rest of our lives. I want us to have a family and—'

She broke off, clamping a hand over her mouth. What

had she said? It was the very bone of contention that had ruined their life together in the first place.

He was smiling as he removed her hand from her mouth and kissed her gently on the lips.

'Darling, that's exactly what I want. I've even bought your dream house in the hope that—'

'My dream house? You mean…?'

He was laughing now, a happy, excited, boyish sound of sheer pleasure.

'Yes, the house you wanted to buy in Cragdale. Don't look so surprised.'

'But how did you…? I mean…'

He pulled her against him. 'Two years ago the house was bought by Freddy Jackson, the consultant who was then in charge of Accident and Emergency. I'm sure you remember him.'

She nodded, trying to come to terms with her feeling of being shell-shocked and ecstatic all at the same time.

'A couple of months ago Freddy took a post in the States so he put his house on the market. I applied for his job and when I got it I also put in a bid for his house. I knew the two-year separation order was coming to an end and that you would have to contact me.'

'And I did,' she breathed. 'Were you hoping that…?'

'I didn't know what to expect, but one thing was for sure. I was going to do my utmost to get us back together again. When you wrote, asking for a meeting over Christmas, I knew I wouldn't have the time to prepare my strategy because of all the work I was committed to here in the hospital. I needed time, time to make plans and time to set the house in order so that I could use it to persuade you.'

'Euan, I don't need any more persuading. When can we see it?'

'How about this afternoon? The central heating has

been switched off during some building repairs but we could light a fire in the sitting room...and in the bedroom.'

'Oh, Euan!' She couldn't express her rapture in mere words.

He put a hand under her chin and tilted her face towards him. 'We'd better talk practicalities. Your work on the cruise ship. How long do you have to be away at any given time?'

'Darling, I'll have to resign my post. I can't leave you for weeks on end!'

He smiled with relief. 'Thank God for that. I was afraid you'd want to keep some of your newfound independence but I didn't want to put pressure on you.'

'My ambition at the moment is to go and see our house and visualise which bedrooms we'll use for our growing family.'

He laughed. 'It's a rambling old place, with room for a whole football team. I forgot to ask if you're still on the Pill.'

She smiled. 'Of course not! I had no reason to be.'

'Then my jealous pangs about lover-boy Richard were unfounded?'

'Absolutely!' She hesitated. 'I'm afraid I was taken totally unprepared tonight and you didn't produce a condom so...'

'I know how you dislike them. I remember that from the early days before you went on the Pill. Anyway, like you, I wasn't prepared for a night of wild, passionate love-making.'

Carol smiled. 'We did a bit of work in between, remember?'

'We did indeed.' He hesitated. 'So our first child may be growing even as we speak.'

She laughed. 'It's a possibility. I'll have to check my dates but I think I'm in the middle of the fertile period.'

'Oh, Carol, I hope so! If not, we'll have to try again and again and...'

'We'd better cancel the divorce proceedings before my solicitor friend gets too involved with it. Janet is an eager beaver.'

'She won't work over Christmas.'

'You don't know Janet! She'll arrive in Wales, have a few hours of family socialising and then get her brief-case out. Which phone shall I use? I'll leave a message on Janet's answerphone. She's the efficient type who will phone in to check her messages from Wales—yes, even on Christmas Day.'

Euan had picked up the bedside phone and was holding it out to her.

'When I've phoned Janet I'd better call the cruise line and check the staffing situation for this next cruise. There won't be a problem. They've always got a list of qualified nurses, longing to take their turn on a world cruise.'

Euan swung his legs over the side of the bed. 'I'd better get ready to face the press, wanting to know about baby Holly's return. They'll be waiting for me in A and E.'

'I'll come with you when I've finished my phone calls.'

He kissed the tip of her nose. 'Don't be long, darling.'

A feeling of euphoria was sweeping over her as she watched Euan disappear into the bathroom.

Dialling Janet's number, she waited for the expected answerphone to click into action.

CHAPTER NINE

CAROL was mystified when Janet answered the phone.

'Janet, what are you doing at home? It's Carol here.'

'I live here, remember?' came the clipped reply.

'But I thought you were on your way to Wales.'

'We should be. Hugh's gone down with this flu that's going around. Kept me awake half the night, moaning about his sore throat and his headache. But the amount of Christmas Eve drink he consumed last night hasn't helped. Anyway, I'm glad of an excuse to catch up with my work. I'm glad you rang because I've just got your file out and—'

'Janet, we don't want to go ahead with the divorce.'

There was silence at the other end. Carol waited a few seconds.

'Janet, are you there?'

'I'm delighted! It's such marvellous news! Congratulations!'

'Thanks.'

Carol smiled at Euan who had just emerged from the bathroom with a large brown towel round his waist as he padded, barefoot, over the carpet towards the chair where his carelessly tossed suit lay sprawled in a wet heap. She watched him take one disgusted look at it, before opening the vast mahogany wardrobe in search of a well-pressed suit.

'So I can put this file in the shredder, can I?' Janet asked.

Carol smiled into the phone. 'Absolutely!'

There was a short pause during which Carol could hear Janet tapping something into her computer.

'Tell me, is there any news of that poor baby who was snatched from the hospital? I saw something about it on the morning news and—'

'We've got her back!' Carol couldn't keep the joy and pride from her voice.

'Marvellous ! How?'

Carol leaned back against the pillows, cradling the phone. 'Oh, it's a long story, Janet.'

Euan, doing up the buttons of a clean shirt with one hand, was making winding motions with the other to indicate that he wanted her to cut it short.

'I've got to go, Janet. Euan and I are about to hold a press conference regarding the kidnapped baby.'

'How exciting! So if I watch the news I'll get the full story?'

Carol hesitated. 'Most of it.'

She was going to be careful about what she said. Poor, misguided Penny's future lay in the balance.

'Thanks for everything, Janet,' she added quickly. 'If you'll send me your bill I'll—'

'I'm not going to charge you a fee, for heaven's sake! All I did was come over to the hospital for a chat. Take it as a Christmas present.'

'Thanks very much. Happy Christmas, Janet!'

She put down the phone.

'Could you leave the cruise line call until after the conference?' Euan said, stooping to fasten the laces on his shoes. We're running a bit late.'

Emerging through the double doors that separated the residents' quarters from the main part of the hospital, Carol could hear the buzz of voices.

'They're here! That's the doctor and the nurse who found the baby!'

Suddenly they were besieged by cameramen and reporters, who crowded round, pushed microphones in front of them and flashed cameras in their faces.

'Just a moment,' Euan said, in his firm, consultant, I'm-in-charge voice. 'Please, will you all move back into the reception area, otherwise I'll have to ask you to leave. It may be Christmas Day but this is a hospital which never closes. We've got important work, taking place, and I will not have it disrupted.'

Carol watched as the over-exuberant press retreated. Out of the corner of her eye she saw Fay, rushing towards them.

'Sorry about that,' she said. 'They were meant to wait for you over there.'

'Fay, why aren't you in bed, asleep?' Carol asked as they followed the press contingent into the waiting room.

Fay shrugged. 'Do you think I could sleep when I knew all this was going on in my department? I snoozed for half an hour and then came back. Janice Watson was delighted to put me in charge of holding back the press so that she could get on with running the department. Anyway, have *you* been to bed yet?'

Carol gave a shy smile. 'You could say that.'

For a couple of seconds Fay glanced from Carol to Euan and then back again. A slow, knowing smile spread across her face.

'Oh, that's wonderful! Then does that mean…?'

Carol nodded. 'Yes, but…'

'Does everybody know?'

'Not yet.'

Fay's face was wreathed in smiles. 'Have you phoned Janet?'

'Of course. We've officially cancelled the divorce.'

'When you two have finished chatting,' Euan put in, 'the press are waiting for us.'

'Congratulations, Euan!' Fay said.

Euan smiled broadly. 'You make it sound as if there's going to be a wedding.'

'Well, why not?' Fay said. 'Yes, I think you should have another wedding. Or at least a big celebration so that... Oh, I nearly forgot. I've got something for you, Carol.'

Fay delved into the pocket of her uniform and produced a small necklace made out of red beads.

'Remember Deirdre, the little girl who pushed a bead in her ear last night?' Fay asked. 'Her father brought this in about half an hour ago.'

'Of course,' Carol said, taking hold of the necklace. 'She promised to make this for me. Isn't it lovely? I'm going to treasure this as a memento of the most wonderful Christmas of my life.'

'The most wonderful Christmas so far,' Euan said quietly. 'There'll be lots more. Come on, we'd better get this show on the road.'

A long table had been placed at one end of the waiting room. Half a dozen patients with minor complaints were sitting at the back of the room, waiting to be seen by Euan's housemen. From the intrigued expression on the patients' faces they were in no hurry to leave this interesting scene.

Rumours about the return of baby Holly had been circulating all morning, and patients and staff alike were anxious to get a ringside view of the press conference.

Fay, Carol and Euan sat down at the long table and the journalists jockeyed for good positions in front of them. The chattering ceased as Obstetrics Sister Patricia Galloway brought in Laurie Gibson in a wheelchair. The young mother was clutching Holly, wrapped in a blanket, holding her as if she would never let go of her again.

Carol leaned forward and spoke quietly to Sister Galloway.

'Shouldn't baby Holly be having her treatment under the blue lamp, Sister?'

The obstetrics sister smiled. 'Don't worry, we've interrupted Holly's treatment for a few minutes only. It won't harm her. The tests we've done show she's improving all the time.'

Carol leaned back, satisfied that Holly was in good hands.

'Can you hold the baby up so we can get a good shot?' one of the cameramen called.

'I'm afraid not,' Euan said firmly. 'You can come up one at a time and take one shot of the baby in her mother's arms, starting with this gentleman here in the front row.'

Carol leapt to her feet and hovered protectively near Laurie and Holly. The young mother looked happy but tired, only the dark rings around her eyes indicating she'd been to hell and back during the night. Holly was sleeping peacefully, the yellow tinge to her skin definitely fainter.

Carol had been trying to keep out of the picture, but one of the photographers asked if she would be photographed.

'You're the nurse who found the baby, aren't you? Let's have a shot of you, leaning over the baby. Just one!' he pleaded.

Carol looked at Euan who nodded resignedly. Carol moved over to Laurie and Holly.

Lights flashed. Carol was sure she'd blinked at the wrong moment.

'And how about one of the doctor who pulled the bogus nurse from the river?' somebody called out.

Euan reluctantly complied, before putting up his hand and announcing that all cameras had to be put away and that baby and mother were going back to the ward to resume treatment.

Carol went back to her seat at the long table. Questions were fired at them from every part of the room. She gave her account as dispassionately as possible.

Euan, too, answered every question that was put to him in a calm, professional manner. He was deliberately evasive about what was to happen to Penny. Some of the press were suggesting that she should be behind bars.

Carol held her breath as she listened to Euan answer that one.

'As medical professionals, it's not our policy to condemn,' he said evenly. 'Penny has been placed in the care of a psychiatrist and will receive treatment.'

'I know what treatment I'd give her!' one of the reporters called out. 'She needs stringing up for what she did to that poor young mother.'

'Penny needs medical help,' Euan said patiently. 'And that's what she'll receive.'

He rose. 'So, now, ladies and gentlemen, if you wouldn't mind dispersing as quietly as you can, we've got a hospital to run. I hope you all have a happy Christmas.'

'Thanks, and the same to you!'

'Happy Christmas, sir.'

'Happy Christmas, Nurse!'

Carol smiled as she stood, acknowledging all the good wishes.

Fay tugged at her sleeve, seeking her attention.

'Aren't you going to announce the happy news?'

'You must be joking!' Carol said vehemently.

'No, I'm not joking.'

Fay was clapping her hands to attract the attention of

the departing press. 'Euan, you're going to make an announcement, aren't you?'

Carol saw a slow smile spread over Euan's handsome face. One moment he'd been the strict consultant and the next he looked like a young student.

The room was quiet again, the reporters and cameramen turning to see what the announcement was going to be.

Euan put out his hand and pulled Carol against him, his arm around her shoulders.

'My wife, Carol, and I have just been through a two-year separation,' he said quietly. 'Don't ask me why because it didn't make sense when we split and it doesn't make sense now. All I know is that my wonderful wife came back into my life on Christmas Eve and I'm the happiest man in the world so...'

Loud cheers drowned the end of Euan's sentence. Carol could feel tears, pricking at the back of her eyes. Out of the corner of her eye she could see Fay, sniffing into a tissue. Glancing up at Euan, she saw a heart-stopping expression of tenderness in his eyes.

She swallowed hard, before whispering, 'I'm so happy!'

'Me, too,' he said in a barely audible, husky voice. 'Let's escape this circus and go back to my room. We've got phone calls to make and then...'

He bent his head and kissed her full on the lips. The cheers erupted once again and cameras flashed.

Euan raised his head, smiling. 'And that, ladies and gentleman, really is the end.'

Pulling her against him as he swept her out of the room, he whispered, 'But for us, my darling, it's only the beginning.'

EPILOGUE

'"TWAS the night before Christmas, when all through the house, not a creature was stirring, not even a mouse,' Euan said from the top of the stepladder as he fixed the fairy on the top of the Christmas tree.

He leaned back to admire his handiwork. 'There! What do you think, Carol?'

Carol, holding the ladder steady, looked up at Euan. 'I think you should come down from that top step before you start leaning back like that.'

She put her head on one side. 'The fairy looks fine, if a bit battered.'

'A bit battered!' Euan said in mock disgust as he rapidly descended the ladder.

His bare feet hardly touched the rungs. He looked relaxed and happy in his ancient, patched-at-the-knees jeans and baggy, navy blue, fisherman's sweater.

'You'd be battered if you'd spent four years in a tin trunk.'

He reached the bottom and put his arm around her waist. 'Instead of which you look absolutely wonderful.'

Carol put a hand up to feel her hair, which hadn't seen a comb for hours. All day she'd been baking mince pies, stuffing the turkey, peeling potatoes, preparing the sprouts and wrapping presents, besides looking after three-month-old baby William.

'I feel an absolute mess,' she said, unrolling the sleeves of her black polo neck sweater and smoothing her crumpled denim skirt. 'What I need most is a long soak in the bath.'

179

His fingers on her waist tightened. 'Good idea! I'll join you.'

She laughed. 'Not until we've finished the tree. The lower branches need—'

'The lower branches can wait,' he said, kissing the tip of her nose. 'It's four years since we had a proper Christmas Eve together and we're going to enjoy ourselves so just relax and take it easy.'

He was taking her into his arms. She gave a sigh of contentment as he obliterated her practical thoughts. His kiss was tender and undemanding. The kiss of a man who was saving himself for later! she thought with a shiver of anticipation.

'Come and sit by the fire and I'll get the champagne,' he said, pulling her over to the large cretonne-covered sofa in front of the wide, open, inglenook fireplace.

Pushing aside the box of baby wipes and the packet of disposable nappies, she leaned back against the squashy cushions as she waited for Euan to return from the kitchen. Through dreamily half-closed eyes, she watched the flames dance over the logs. One of the logs fell onto the hearth. She picked up the tongs and tossed it back into the centre of the fire. Sparks flew up the chimney.

She gave a sigh of contentment. What a different situation she was in from last Christmas Eve, when she'd arrived at Moortown General for a spell of night duty. Little had she known that all her dreams had been about to come true!

She looked up at the mass of Christmas cards, adorning the mantelpiece. There had been so many cards this year that they'd had to string them across the oak beams that traversed the ceilings of their sixteenth-century house. Even Richard had sent them a card from

Singapore, where the cruise ship was spending Christmas.

He'd enclosed a short letter, saying that he hoped everything was working out for them and that Carol wasn't getting itchy feet. Itchy feet. What a cheek! The thought that she might have been miles away on the cruise ship instead of here in her cosy home with Euan and William was too awful to contemplate.

There had been no problem with the cruise line when she'd resigned, she remembered. The directors had sent their congratulations. And her post had been swiftly snapped up by some lucky applicant.

She glanced round the room and her eyes rested for a moment on the brightly lit Christmas tree, the lower branches groaning with Christmas presents. She hadn't closed the long, heavy, crimson damask curtains over the window this evening, and through the window she could see a crescent moon, shining down on Cragdale.

From where she was sitting she could just make out the other side of the valley. Pinpricks of light punctuated the velvety darkness. One of those pinpricks represented the cottage where she was born.

Moving into this beautiful old house had been like coming home, only different. It was the home she'd always wanted, a home full of love and laughter. And the arrival of William had made everything complete.

Euan placed the ice bucket on the side table next to her. She looked up and smiled.

'Is it really four years since we had a real Christmas Eve together?'

Euan, busying himself with the cork, nodded. 'Four years ago, the first Christmas of our marriage, we had a wonderful time. Three years ago we had a row and you decided to walk out on me, two years ago we were apart and last Christmas Eve we were on duty—remember?'

'How could I ever forget?'

She took hold of the champagne flute he was holding out to her. 'Mustn't drink more than a glassful. I don't want William to get tipsy on his first Christmas.'

Euan laughed. 'Only about ten per cent gets through to the baby so don't worry. Happy Christmas, darling!'

He clinked his glass against hers as he sat on the sofa, one arm loosely over her shoulders.

'Last year was a memorable Christmas Eve in more ways than one,' Euan said, staring into the flames of the fire as if visualising the events.

Carol took a sip of champagne. 'I'll never forget that press conference! When you insisted on announcing that we were together again, I—'

'I wanted the whole world to share the good news!'

'The whole world and your mother!'

Euan laughed. 'Especially my mother. There'd been enough pretence about our marriage. It was time to come clean.'

She snuggled against him. 'I remember she was a bit shocked when she saw that picture of our kiss splashed all over the front page of her morning paper.'

'She got over it, especially when a couple of months later we told her there was a baby on the way.'

'She adores William. I had to persuade her that I could cope on my own today or she would have been over here like a shot.'

She looked up enquiringly at Euan. 'Do you think your parents like their new cottage? Your mother's always complaining it's too near the river. It's bound to be damp, she says.'

Euan laughed. 'My mother likes having something to complain about. She wouldn't be happy if she couldn't complain. Dad told me they've never been happier since we moved them down here. I must admit I didn't think they'd ever leave Scotland, but as soon as they knew there was a grandchild on the way there was no holding them.'

'Amazing what a difference a baby makes! Which reminds me, have you heard how Penny is?'

'She's still a patient of Hugh Farmer, having psychiatric treatment. He's quietly confident she's making progress, but she's got a long way to go.'

'And baby Holly? She'll be a year old tonight, won't she?'

'I saw Holly and her mother in Outpatients the other day. They call her in for routine checks every month, just to make sure she's suffered no ill-effects from the abduction. She's a lovely baby. She was crawling all over the floor and pulling herself up, trying to walk. A real bundle of joy she is...'

He paused, listening. 'Talking of which, isn't that our own little bundle of joy calling out for attention?'

'He'll be hungry again. I'll go and feed him.'

She started gathering up the wipes and nappies.

Euan topped up the two champagne flutes. 'I'll come with you and run the bath for after the feed.'

'There's still lots to do downstairs. I'd like to set the table for tomorrow. There'll be Cousin Brenda and her husband, your mum and dad, Fay and her new boyfriend and—'

'I'll set the table in the morning,' Euan said, taking a firm hold of her arm.

He reached across to put the wrought-iron fireguard in front of the log fire.

Carol ran up the stairs, Euan following with the champagne. William was lying on his back, kicking his legs in the air and howling loudly. As soon as Carol leaned over the cot he stopped and gave her an angelic smile.

She reached down to smooth back the blond hair from his forehead. He was so like his dad!

Big blue eyes stared up at her, willing her to pick him up.

'There, he's not hungry at all,' Euan said, his arm round Carol's shoulders.

'Oh, but he is,' she said, gathering William into her arms and settling herself on the low feeding chair before pulling up her sweater.

Euan dropped a kiss on his son's blond head. Baby William gurgled in response as his little rosebud mouth latched onto Carol.

'I'll run the bath. Don't be long, Carol.'

Euan paused in the doorway and looked back at his wife and son.

Carol looked up and gave him a blissful smile. 'Happy Christmas, Euan.'

He blew her a kiss. 'Happy Christmas, darling.'

MILLS & BOON®

Makes any time special

Enjoy a romantic novel from
Mills & Boon®

Presents™   Enchanted™   Temptation®

Historical Romance™   Medical Romance™

MILLS & BOON®

Next Month's Romance Titles

♡

Each month you can choose from a wide variety of romance novels from Mills & Boon®. Below are the new titles to look out for next month from the Presents™ and Enchanted™ series.

Presents™

TO WOO A WIFE	Carole Mortimer
CONTRACT BABY	Lynne Graham
IN BED WITH THE BOSS	Susan Napier
SURRENDER TO SEDUCTION	Robyn Donald
OUTBACK MISTRESS	Lindsay Armstrong
THE SECRET DAUGHTER	Catherine Spencer
THE MARRIAGE ASSIGNMENT	Alison Kelly
WIFE BY AGREEMENT	Kim Lawrence

Enchanted™

BE MY GIRL!	Lucy Gordon
LONESOME COWBOY	Debbie Macomber
A SUITABLE GROOM	Liz Fielding
NEW YEAR...NEW FAMILY	Grace Green
OUTBACK HUSBAND	Jessica Hart
MAKE-BELIEVE MOTHER	Pamela Bauer & Judy Kaye
OH, BABY!	Lauryn Chandler
FOLLOW THAT GROOM!	Christie Ridgway

On sale from 8th January 1999

HI 9812

Available at most branches of WH Smith, Tesco, Asda, Martins, Borders and all good paperback bookshops

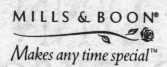

MILLS & BOON®

Makes any time special™

By Request™

Bestselling themed romances brought back to you by popular demand

Each month By Request brings you three full-length novels in one beautiful volume featuring the best of the best.

So if you missed a favourite Romance the first time around, here is your chance to relive the magic from some of our most popular authors.

Look out for
***Blind Passions* in January 1999 featuring Miranda Lee, Rebecca Winters and Emma Goldrick**

Available at most branches of WH Smith, Tesco, Asda, Martins, Borders, Easons, Volume One/James Thin and most good paperback bookshops

LYNN ERICKSON

The Eleventh Hour

Jack Devlin is on Death Row, convicted of murdering his
beautiful socialite wife. But the evidence is too cut and dry
for lawyer Eve Marchand. When Jack escapes and
contacts Eve, she is forced to make a decision that
changes her life.

*"Lynn Erickson joins the ranks of Sandra Brown
and Nora Roberts"*

—The Paperback Forum

1-55166-426-7
**AVAILABLE IN PAPERBACK
FROM DECEMBER, 1998**

We are giving away a year's supply of Mills & Boon® books to the five lucky winners of our latest competition. Simply match the six film stars to the films in which they appeared, complete the coupon overleaf and send this entire page to us by 30th June 1999. The first five correct entries will each win a year's subscription to the Mills & Boon series of their choice. What could be easier?

CABARET	___	GONE WITH THE WIND	___
ROCKY	___	SMOKEY & THE BANDIT	___
PRETTY WOMAN	___	GHOST	___

C8L

Please turn over for details of how to enter ➜

HOW TO ENTER

There are six famous faces and a list of six films overleaf. Each of the famous faces starred in one of the films listed and all you have to do is match them up!

As you match each one, write the number of the actor or actress who starred in each film in the space provided. When you have matched them all, fill in the coupon below, pop this page in an envelope and post it today. Don't forget you could win a year's supply of Mills & Boon® books—you don't even need to pay for a stamp!

Mills & Boon Hollywood Heroes Competition
FREEPOST CN81, Croydon, Surrey, CR9 3WZ
EIRE readers: (please affix stamp) PO Box 4546, Dublin 24.

Please tick the series you would like to receive if you
are one of the lucky winners

Presents™ ❑   Enchanted™ ❑   Historical Romance™ ❑

Medical Romance™ ❑   Temptation® ❑

Are you a Reader Service™ subscriber?   Yes ❑   No ❑

Ms/Mrs/Miss/Mr ....Initials ....
                                                    (BLOCK CAPITALS PLEASE)

Surname...

Address ....

....

...................................Postcode...........................

(I am over 18 years of age)   C8L

Closing date for entries is 30th June 1999. One entry per household. Free subscriptions are for four books per month. Competition open to residents of the UK and Ireland only. As a result of this application, you may receive further offers from Harlequin Mills & Boon and other carefully selected companies. If you would prefer not to share in this opportunity please write to The Data Manager at the address shown above.

Mills & Boon is a registered trademark of
Harlequin Mills & Boon Ltd.